COMES TO THE
MIDDLE KINGDOM
VOL. 1 – 1939-1942

Cover illustrations and sketches by
Al Musso

WAR
COMES TO THE
MIDDLE KINGDOM
VOL. 1 – 1939-1942

Armed Forces Day parade in San Luis Obispo, 1942. *Photo courtesy of San Luis Obispo County Historical Museum.*

Edited by

Stan Harth • Liz Krieger • Dan Krieger
for the San Luis Obispo County Historical Society

EZ Nature Books
San Luis Obispo, California

ISBN 0-945092-24-5

Dedicated to
BARBARA PARKER CITLAU
and all those who served on the Home Front
—and to the docents who, like Barbara, maintain the front line at
the San Luis Obispo County Historical Museum.

Barbara Parker Citlau worked in the Camp San Luis Obispo Utilities Office at the beginning of this war. Barbara served as Director of Docents for the San Luis Obispo County Historical Museum from 1980 to 1990. *This photo, which is by courtesy of San Luis Obispo City-County Library, first appeared in SHOT 'N SHELL, the Camp San Luis Obispo newspaper, on March 27, 1942.*

PREFACE AND ACKNOWLEDGEMENTS
by Dan Krieger

Charles Beard wrote that "written history is an act of faith." Written history is also the only mechanism through which we can at least initiate a debate on what happened in the past.

Over the past eight years, I've published a weekly column, "Times Past," on California and Central Coast history for the *San Luis Obispo County Telegram-Tribune*. Occasionally, readers have written to cite my more grievous errors. More frequently, they have made comments which substantially enhance my knowledge and understanding of the subject at hand. I'm able to pass these benefits along in future columns.

In 1981, the editors of this volume worked with Eleanor and Patrick Brown to produce an issue of *La Vista: The Journal of Central Coast History (Vol. 4, No.2)* subtitled *San Luis Obispo Goes to War, 1939-1945*. That journal sold out in a matter of days, and a second printing was necessary. It is now a collector's item.

Once again Stan Harth has served as project superintendent and critical editor. Deadlines simply would not have been met without Stan as the driving force. Liz Krieger collected much of the original research.

As was the case in 1981, the San Luis Obispo County Historical Museum's collections were critical to our research. The volunteer docents and staff worked tirelessly to provide the information and photographs we needed.

The staff of the San Luis Obispo City-County Library has provided much assistance. We are especially grateful to Virginia Crook, Lynn Wiech, Morgan Philbin and Margaret Price. Marjory Johnson, Paula Ogren and Professor Art Hansen of Cal State, Fullerton, did critical readings of various parts of the manuscript. M.Eugene Smith, Emeritus Professor of History at Cal Poly, was an invaluable resource on the history of the war-impacted college.

We are also grateful to Dr. Robert E. Kennedy, President Emeritus of Cal Poly, and his wife, Mary, for the hours of conversation and written notes which help us to better understand the history of present day San Luis Obispo's principal business.

A.G. and Helen Drum Wilson helped us clarify many details of wartime history in several interviews.

Bill Cattaneo, whose fine understanding of the 1930s and 1940s is transmitted daily through his "Our Town" broadcasts, has been a constant source of information, reference checking and photographs.

The following individuals and groups were of invaluable assistance in our earlier studies and have contributed to the success of this volume:

Zaidee Andrews; the Atascadero Historical Society; Cliff and Marge Boswell; Gordon Bennett; Bill Callaway; the Special Collections Department at the Robert E. Kennedy Library, California Polytechnic State University, and its unfailingly helpful staff—Bob Blesse (now Director of Special Collections at the University of Nevada, Reno), Sherry Smith and Dottie Stechman, Reference Librarians Paul Adalian, Lane Paige, Doug Gates and Glenn Whaley; Enid and Arthur B. Eddy; Woody Frey; Elsa Orcutt Hewitt; Peter Andre; Helen Foree Keller; Lucille Kimball; Tillie Lacterman; Stella Louis; Pearl Mallagh; Neva Mae Negranti Nogle; Emily Hoffman McGinn; Elsie Muzio; Betty Righetti Middlecamp; Marj Mackey; Clark Herman; Patrick Nagano; Sarah Nadelle; Rose Jones; Ralph and Sylvia Vorhies; Ellen Newsom; Harvey Norton; Cecile O'Donnell; Virginia Peterson of Paso Robles; Howard Stornetta; Arnold and Peggy Teague; the *San Luis Obispo County Telegram-Tribune* and staff members Dorie Bentley, John Frees, Ann Fairbanks, Warren Groshong, Wayne Nichols and Bob Nichols; Jim Hayes and Tony Hertz who were working at the *Telegram-Tribune* in 1981; the *Morro Bay Sun-Bulletin*; George DeBord, editor emeritus of both the *Telegram-Tribune* and the *Sun Bulletin*, who has been a constant source of friendship and encouragement; George Brand, editor emeritus of the *Telegram-Tribune* and current editor of *Senior Magazine*; Frank Tanaka of Long Beach; Dorothy Hoover Thomson; Tracy Conway; Ruth Lenger; Arlene Villa Zanchuck; Jean Seitz; Susie Eto Kikuchi Bauman and Grace Eto Shibata.

Thanks to all those who generously agreed to be interviewed and who wrote or contributed an article to this book. Their names are in the text. Our profound apologies and thanks go to those we may have accidentally omitted in this journey through our county's lively past.

We would particularly like to thank the thoughtful, hard working directors of the museum, including Gary Hoving, Marj Johnson, Jerry Doser, Ralph Vorhies, Bill Froom, Betty Clarke and Barbara Citlau.

Finally, special thanks to Jo Harth for her love and encouragement.

We also have been able to greatly increase the photo documentation at the County Historical Museum through the capable work of the late director, Lura Rawson, and Mark Hall-Patton, the current director. In 1986, Lura began writing a weekly history column for the North County Supplement of the *San Luis Obispo County Telegram-Tribune*. In 1987, Mark began his column for the South County Supplement. Thus, the San Luis Obispo County Historical Society was able to reach the far corners of our

The City of San Luis Obispo—circa 1940—as seen from San Luis Mountain. *Photo courtesy of San Luis Obispo County Historical Museum.*

region. This has resulted in marvelous feedback on a variety of subjects, including the epoch of the Second World War.

If you have memories or information pertaining to the period after March of 1942, the very loose "cut-off" date for this tome, please let us know in sufficient time for *Volume II*, which will treat the period from March of 1942 to the end of the war in August of 1945. We plan that publication for mid-1992.

A future history is planned dealing with the Korean War era and after.

INTRODUCTION

California's south-central coastal area still seems a bit removed from the hustle and bustle of world events. That's part of the attraction of northern Santa Barbara County and San Luis Obispo County. So we've taken the liberty of calling this region "The Middle Kingdom."

Its isolation was far greater before December of 1941. Hitler's *Anschluss* of his native Austria and the disastrous appeasement at Munich, the blitzkrieg assault on Poland, the fall of France and the evacuation at Dunkirk all seemed so far away from the small towns and cattle and dairy farms nestled among the rolling hills.

Most Middle Kingdom residents were only hazily aware that the War Department was concerned over the likelihood of hostilities with Japan and was intent on increasing the strength of coastal defenses by constructing training bases from Fort Lewis in Washington to the Marine Corps' Camp Pendleton in Southern California.

Because Santa Barbara and San Luis Obispo Counties had excellent transportation links with the major port cities and urban centers of the Pacific coast, a number of military training facilities were developed within their boundaries.

Camp Roberts and Camp San Luis Obispo, both in San Luis Obispo County, were two of the largest training camps in the United States. Even a sleepy fishing port like Morro Bay was awarded a naval base.

The rugged terrain between Point Conception and Point Arguello was ideal for "toughening up" troops bound for the invasion of Italy, France and, if necessary, the Japanese home islands. And so the government leased and purchased the greater portion of several Mexican land grants for Camp Cooke.

The flatland surrounding Santa Maria and Paso Robles seemed ideal for airfields. Captain Allan G. Hancock had begun a flying school in Santa Maria in the late 1920's. The future Hancock College was nationalized for the duration. A second airfield was constructed southwest of Santa Maria. It eventually became home to squadrons of Lockheed P-38s—the double fuselage, long-range fighter planes that brought a final end to Germany's superiority in the air.

Paso Robles also became home to two airfields, one of which continues to serve as a mainstay in the battles against California's forest and brush fires.

The federal government moved in swiftly, leasing and buying up land as early as February of 1940. Few residents were aware of the changes that were in store for them.

San Luis Obispans seemed ready to accept the inevitability of change. For example, Louis Sinsheimer had been a popular and highly regarded mayor of San Luis Obispo since 1919. He was opposed to growth and change and kept the public debt low. However, the city's streets, water and sewer systems were in desperate need of modernization. In 1939, Fred Kimball, an automobile dealer, was elected as the new mayor. He would confront problems far greater than rusting water mains during his wartime tenure in office.

The California Polytechnic Institute at San Luis Obispo was gearing up for its first four year collegiate degree programs in 1939. But its director, Julian A. McPhee, also looked to the future. At the request of the Civil Aeronautics Authority, McPhee authorized 72 hours of ground maintenance instruction and 35 hours of flight training by licensed pilots at San Luis Obispo's airport.

Cal Poly also instituted programs under the National Youth Authority Resident Project and the Adult National Defense Training Program. The school provided emergency training for some 3,500 men and women.

Meanwhile, a bit of the European war came to the Paso Robles region. Ignace Paderewski, a famed pianist and the first president of the Polish Republic, had returned to his San Ygnacio Ranch northwest of Paso Robles. After the fall of Poland in September of 1939, Paderewski and his wife hosted dances at the Paso Robles Hotel to raise funds for the Free Poles who were regrouping in the British Isles.

Ron Dunin, a future mayor of San Luis Obispo, was among the Poles who escaped from their German conquerors and made their way to England.

Some young Central Coast residents were already in action. Frank Avila, the son of a Portuguese ranching family from the Pismo Beach area, went on to attend U.C.L.A. in the late 1930's. He read about the Fascist atrocities in Spain during that nation's traumatic Civil War. As Fascism began to envelop Europe after September of 1939, Frank enlisted in the United States Navy. Pearl Harbor found him in our Mediterranean Fleet. Frank was transferred to the Pacific and went on to become the military and civilian administrator of the Marshall and Mariana Islands.

Heavy rains began to fall along coastal California in December of 1940. It rained almost continuously through April. Most of the military facilities were scheduled to receive troops in March of 1941. The rains slowed construction to a standstill. An average of more than 42 inches of rain fell over the region. Railroad tracks, culverts and bridges were washed out. Heavy equipment was made useless, isolated in mud-soaked fields. Much of the completed construction was destroyed.

On Aug. 14, 1941, the *San Luis Obispo Telegram-Tribune's* headlines shouted: "U.S. SENATE GROUP ATTACKS CAMP ABOUT BUILDING COSTS." Harry S Truman, the junior senator from Missouri, would make a name for himself investigating the enormous cost overruns at Camp San Luis.

A number of good things came from the construction of the camps. The Great Depression had hit California both hard and late. Tens of thousands of men flocked to the Central Coast in search of jobs that paid a federally guaranteed 65¢ an hour.

In June of 1941, construction was begun on the Rinconada Dam on the upper Salinas River. The dam forms what is now Santa Margarita Lake and still supplies a substantial portion of the water needs of the city of San Luis Obispo.

Meanwhile, San Luis Obispo went "big time" with its first modern bus system. The green buses of Jones Transportation Company began operating over regularly scheduled routes on June 20, 1941. After the war, the bus system vanished and wasn't resurrected until the mid-1970's!

Some city residents were mildly shocked by an "All Girl Taxicab Business" reported by the *San Luis Obispo Independent* on July 11, 1941.

And in September of 1941, the City of San Luis Obispo put up its first four-way signs with street names, presumably to help all the new strangers in town.

The housing crunch was very real as workers for the camps and military dependents sought places to stay. Wives, girlfriends and sometimes even mothers and fathers came to be near their husbands, boyfriends and sons who had arrived at the camps. As early as Jan. 11, 1941, the *Telegram-Tribune* reported that "A man with $160 in ten dollar bills came to the Police Station and begged for a place to stay. He said he was unable to find a bed in town for the night. He was given a 'Sleeper' there."

Steve Zegar was San Luis Obispo's longtime cabby. He had achieved fame by providing a link between William Randolph Hearst's rail siding off California Boulevard in San Luis Obispo and the Hearst Ranch at San Simeon. War preparedness made Steve's life a bit easier. Since 1919, Steve had to get out of his cab in all sorts of weather and open the gates of the cattle fences which blocked the circuitous Morro Road that stretched through the Chorro Valley. Once through, he had to get out of the cab and lock the gate behind him.

In January of 1942, the *Telegram-Tribune* reported that "everyone beamed when it was revealed that the Morro Road, between the city and the camp, was to become a four-lane highway. Congress just voted $630,000 to do the job." This short section was the first four-lane highway to be constructed between Los Angeles and San Jose.

The downside for Steve was that Mr. Hearst and his guests wouldn't be taking many trips to San Simeon for the duration.

On Dec. 6, 1941, a small headline in the *Telegram-Tribune* noted **"COUNTY WILL OBSERVE FOR AIR ATTACK."** Under the headline, the newspaper reported that "as part of a state-wide test, 50 observation posts throughout the county" would be manned by crews of about ten persons each for five days. The exercise would help determine the county's ability to spot enemy aircraft.

When the plans were executed several weeks after Sunday, December 7th, they were very much for real.

War actually came to The Middle Kingdom with the sinking of the *Montebello*, a Union Oil tanker, off north county shores in late December of 1941. This torpedoing was among the first effects of the Second World War to touch directly upon the shores of the continental United States.

That war would take the lives of young men from The Middle Kingdom. Lt. Col. Cornelius J. Norton was killed while training with the 31st Fighter Reconnaissance Squadron in Louisiana before Pearl Harbor. Many more would die.

The war forever changed the lives of almost everyone. This was especially true of the Japanese-American residents of the Central Coast. Northern Santa Barbara and San Luis Obispo Counties were primarily agricultural in 1941. Japanese had lived in this area since the beginning of the 20th century. Their fate was to be intimately tied to the fortunes of war.

But nothing ends without the hope of a new beginning. Hundreds of new residents came to The Middle Kingdom because of the war. Some were escaping from the Nazi onslaught at war's beginning. These refugees are also a part of our story.

—Dan Krieger
Past-President of the San Luis Obispo County Historical Society,
Professor of History, California Polytechnic State University

CONTENTS

OVERVIEW

The Central Coast's association with American wars began during the Revolutionary epoch. In 1778, France and Spain entered into an alliance with the American colonies in their revolt against England.

Spain levied a special tax to pay for that war. Mission San Luis Obispo was taxed approximately $300.

During the Mexican-American War, John C. Frémont passed through San Luis Obispo. While occupying the Old Mission, Frémont spared the life of Don José de Jesus Pico. Pardoning the popular caballero earned Frémont the respect of the Californios. General Andrés Pico would surrender only to Frémont. The two met and negotiated an armistice at Cahuenga Pass in January of 1847. The capitulation at Cahuenga marked the end of those hostilities in California.

During the Civil War, cinnabar ore mines in the Cambria and Adelaida regions were used to make fulminate of mercury for the percussion caps on Union rifles. Quicksilver from the Santa Lucia Mountains was also used to extract gold and silver from the mines of the Mother Lode and Comstock Lode. This helped pay for the costs of that war.

During the First World War, San Luis Obispo became a strategic center. The 120-mile-long Union Oil pipeline brought crude oil from the fields of the San Joaquín Valley to the wharf at Port San Luis. When America declared war on Germany in April of 1917, troops were brought in to guard the Union Oil Wharf at Avila.

The region's contribution to the war included beans. During the pre-refrigeration era, navy beans were the most common military commodity. Prices rose, with U.S. Government subsidies, from less than two cents a pound to as high as 33 cents. Most of the farmers of the Los Osos,

Central Coast's Role in Wars Traced to the U.S. Revolution

Edna, Avila, Huasna, Arroyo Grande and Santa Maria Valleys turned to navy bean production. The Central Coast was famous for beans. Legumes went to feed the doughboys in Flanders. San Luis Obispo's beans also went to feed the starving families of German-occupied Belgium under the auspices of Herbert Hoover's War Relief Agency.

Atascadero founder E.G. Lewis built fruit drying sheds to produce dried fruit which would be purchased under federally-subsidized prices.

Central Coast farmers did quite well, thanks to wartime prices.

The region's experience during the First World War portended later events. Many county residents bore German names. These families were sometimes the subject of bigotry operating under the guise of patriotism.

Patrick Brown recalls what happened to "Granny" Berkemeyer: "Granny" ran a bakery on Higuera Street. One day, Patrick found his mother in a teary state. Seven-year-old Patrick asked what the trouble was. His mother said that she had just been downtown where she heard "Granny" being subjected to all sorts of verbal abuse for "being German."

Marie Schwafel Hinterman's family was Volgadeutsch—they were ethnic Germans who had lived in Russia for over a hundred years before emigrating to the United States. Marie's father was a popular shoemaker. Nonetheless, Mr. Schwafel was harassed by some local "toughs" because of his German name.

Some members of the Sinsheimer family changed their name to Sinton.

The same prejudices which would later affect Japanese-American residents afflicted German-Americans in 1917-18.

—*Dan Krieger*

Places and Events of

WORLD WAR II

IN THE MIDDLE KINGDOM

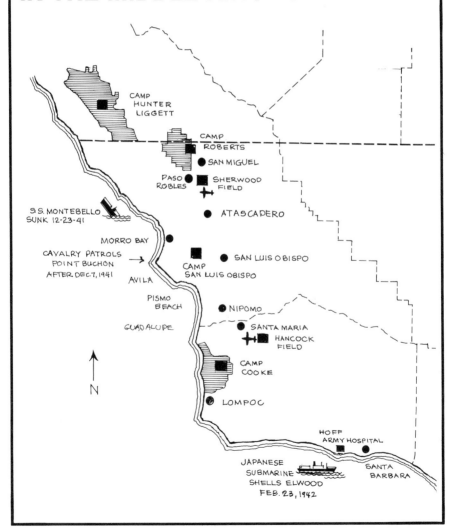

CAMP HUNTER LIGGETT

CAMP ROBERTS

● SAN MIGUEL

PASO ROBLES ● ■ SHERWOOD FIELD

S.S. MONTEBELLO SUNK 12-23-41

● ATASCADERO

MORRO BAY ●

CAVALRY PATROLS POINT BUCHON AFTER DEC.7, 1941 →

CAMP SAN LUIS OBISPO

● SAN LUIS OBISPO

AVILA

PISMO BEACH

● NIPOMO

GUADALUPE

● SANTA MARIA ✈ ■ HANCOCK FIELD

■ CAMP COOKE

N ↑

● LOMPOC

HOFF ARMY HOSPITAL ■

JAPANESE SUBMARINE SHELLS ELWOOD FEB. 23, 1942

● SANTA BARBARA

Part 1

SCHOOLS OF WAR

Al Davis, Camp Historian, and Douglas J. Gates, Cal Poly Library

CAMP ROBERTS GREW FAST AFTER DELAY OF 40 YEARS

"**G**iant piles of lumber occupied a two-block area around the Southern Pacific Depot along Main Street in San Miguel. Day and night, huge trucks would come by and pick up lumber in a feverish attempt to build nearby Camp Roberts. There was so much activity in town then that we had to employ 13 clerks in Eddy's General Merchandise Store while the camp was being built."

So said Enid Eddy, who lived in San Miguel prior to and during World War II.

All of that activity began in November of 1940. It might have happened, although on a smaller scale, 40 years before.

Camp Roberts, which was the largest military training reservation in the United States during World War II, is along the El Camino Real (Highway 101) north of San Miguel. It is where 436,000 men received their military training.

Construction of the camp and the large number of soldiers who went through it had a profound effect on the peaceful and rural communities of San Miguel and Paso Robles.

Before the arrival of the Europeans, the oak-studded, hilly grass lands were occupied by Native Americans (probably Salinan). With bountiful game, sufficient water and a mild climate, they subsisted for centuries by hunting and gathering. They probably were not disturbed by early Spanish explorers, but once the missions were established, their quiet way of life was doomed.

Because of the excellent grazing, the hills surrounding the San Miguel Mission were soon covered with cattle. The hides, or "California bank notes," made the mission prosperous. This aroused jealousy among other Californios. Pressure was applied which led to the secularization of the missions. Their vast holdings were given in the form of land grants to those who curried favor with Mexican government officials.

El Rancho Nacimiento grant, part of which was to become Camp Roberts, was acquired by George Flint. He built his ranch house with stables, barns, corrals and rodeo grounds about five miles west of San Miguel along what was the actual El Camino Real traveled by the priests between Missions San Miguel and San Antonio.

Troops arrived by train at San Miguel and were transported by truck to Camp Roberts. *Photo courtesy of Enid and Arthur Eddy.*

San Miguel's business district hummed with activity. Eddy's General Merchandise, at left, had 13 clerks. *Photo courtesy of Enid and Arthur Eddy.*

The ranch was sold to A.F. Benton, who later resold it to Baron Henry Von Schroeder, a German who also owned Eagle Ranch west of Atascadero. One of the last civilian owners of the ranch was I. W. Hellman, who bought it in 1912.

That purchase followed a period in which the property first was considered a site for military training. For on November 11, 1900, some 40 years before the construction of Camp Roberts started, the Army published Special Order No. 261. This stated the intent of Congress to survey lands suitable for four new Army camps, including one in California.

Those in California included the Nacimiento, Santa Margarita and J. H. Henry (now a portion of the City of Atascadero) Ranches in San Luis Obispo County and the Conejo Ranch in Santa Barbara County.

Under a February 3, 1901, act of Congress during the administration of Theodore Roosevelt, a board was appointed for the survey.

At first it was decided that "the Nacimiento," as the site was then called, was suitable for "a camp for one regiment of cavalry." The report said that the land was compact and had an abundance of water in three fine streams and a fine stand of timber.

Considerable correspondence from the owners of the other prospective sites to the government delayed action until March 1, 1902, when the Chief of Engineers ordered a further survey. Sites for the artillery and rifle ranges were deemed satisfactory. The land was assessed at $5.76 per acre.

The report of May 13, 1902, on climate stated: " The locality is probably as healthy as any in the State of California".

The report continued: "Transportation to camp would have to be via Southern Pacific Railroad from San Francisco to Bradley or San Miguel, about 200 miles; or by ocean steamer to Port Harford, 228 miles, thence by narrow gauge railroad to San Luis Obispo, 10 miles, thence to San Miguel, 46 miles or a total distance of 284 miles."

The Chief of Engineers concurred in the report and recommended the site to Secretary of War Elihu Root.

Dr. John L.D. Roberts, founder of Seaside in Monterey County, wrote a scathing letter to President Roosevelt in which he described the area as being unfit and a "cruel injustice to our soldiers...." He referred to alkaline water, wind storms, desert heat and epidemics.

That letter, and correspondence from residents of San Miguel and Paso Robles who challenged it, caused tremendous repercussions in Washington, D.C. Eventually, the Surgeon General asked the College of Agriculture, University of California, for a report in an attempt to get the matter resolved.

In January of 1904, San Francisco newspapers reported that General

Arthur MacArthur, the father of Douglas MacArthur of World War II fame, appointed a board of medical officers to study the issue. It favored the J. H. Henry Ranch.

The issue went before the House Committee on Military Affairs, whose chairman was reputed to be related to the owner of the Henry Ranch. The Henry Ranch would have cost $504,070, while $360,000 would have covered the Nacimiento Ranch.

The California Congressional delegation was committed to the Nacimiento Ranch; its deadlock with the committee chairman probably caused the proposed facility to be located in another state.

For almost four decades after that decision, the Nacimiento remained a ranch rather than a military installation. Then on September 26, 1940, headlines in the *Paso Robles Press* said: "Great Concentrations Of Troops May Be Based Near Paso Robles" and "U.S. Army Officials Negotiate For The Sites." The newspaper estimated on that date that more than 80,000 troops of cavalry, infantry, artillery and National Guard would be stationed in San Luis Obispo and Monterey Counties.

The Paso Robles Chamber of Commerce, under the presidency of Paul Turner, planned a welcoming event for the troops.

On November 7, 1940, the lease for the 37,000-acre Nacimiento Ranch was completed. Four hundred and fifty acres were reserved for ranching by the Hellman Estate. Vaughn Miller remained as the ranch foreman.

The original date for completion of the camp was to be March 15, 1941, but this was extended when plans for the Artillery Brigade to house 5,000 men south of Bradley were announced on Nov. 21, 1940. The date was then set as July 15, 1941. The estimated cost of the total project was $10,000,000.

San Miguel welcomed the new project, as did the other surrounding communities. Bert Turnbow, a real estate agent in San Miguel, commented that highway lots that were selling for $200 in August were selling for $100 *per foot* in November. Residential lots that had been difficult to sell for $50 now went for as much as $500. The *Paso Robles Press* of March 27, 1941, reported, "Rents on Highway 101 have been hiked from $15 a month to as high as $300."

This type of gouging was eliminated when the federal government rolled back prices to preconstruction levels. Prices of other commodities also were frozen, but several store owners managed to amass sizable fortunes because of the volume of business. During some periods, shopkeepers would not bother to stock shelves, leaving their customers to select what they wanted from opened boxes.

The boom town atmosphere also was seen at the bank. Bank of

America, the only bank then in Paso Robles, opened a branch at the camp to facilitate financial transactions for the construction workers and the soldiers. Allen Peterson, a bank employee at the time, recalled how crowds would wait at the door for the bank to open. He said there were few problems with bad checks.

However, bank officials were concerned about the possible theft of payrolls that were shipped by rail from San Francisco. When the train departed, it would have as much as $5,000,000 on board to be delivered to Fort Ord and Camps Roberts and San Luis. The trains had many guards, and elaborate precautions were taken. No attempt was made to rob a train.

Serious crime was not a major problem, probably because of a sense of urgency about the war effort. Anyone who broke the law to line his own pockets would be considered unpatriotic. There was some problem with so-called victimless crimes such as prostitution and gambling, and a group of ministers criticized law enforcement agencies for being too lax. Some brothels were shut down, but many of the prostitutes operated from their automobiles.

Drunk drivers also were a problem, particularly because Highway 101 was comprised of only two lanes.

All of these developments occurred as the construction workers and then the soldiers arrived. They started when Captain J. T. Smoody arrived in Paso Robles as the representative of the government to oversee all construction. Smoody, a Reserve Officer, was a member of the Construction Quartermaster Corps, which at that time did all the construction for the Army. His original staff consisted of five officers and 75 civilians.

The government awarded the design contract to Holmes and Narver Co. of Los Angeles and the actual construction to the Morrison-Knudsen Construction Co. and the Ford J. Twaits Co.

Subcontractors for the project were: J. Herman & Co., heating for all living quarters; H. S. McClellen, heat for the other buildings; Main Cornice Works, sheet metal work; Newbery Electric Co., electrical work, and Lomin Brothers, plumbing and steam heat.

Temporary offices for the contractors and the Quartermaster were in the upper stories of the Bank of America in Paso Robles. Initially, many of those involved in the project resided at the Paso Robles Inn, but it burned to the ground on December 12, 1940. All 25 rooms of the Bressler Hotel in San Miguel were also leased to the contracting firms.

Construction was planned on six tracts of leased land. Two of the largest tracts were the Nacimiento and the Porter-Sesnon Ranches. The land was leased to the government on an annual basis for a period of five years. The Nacimiento was leased for $125,000 for the first year and $60,000 per

Construction underway during a rare dry day at Camp Roberts. *Photo courtesy of Al Davis.*

Heavy rains slowed the project. *Photo courtesy of Al Davis.*

Tents served as offices for construction bosses during the project. *Photo courtesy of Al Davis.*

year thereafter. The Porter-Sesnon Ranch of 8,174 acres was leased for $6 per acre for the first six months, $5 per acre for the next year and $3 per acre thereafter. That lease had a clause that excluded the firing of live ammunition. All the leases had purchase clauses.

Establishing the actual boundaries of the properties involved proved quite difficult because, for the most part, they were based on surveys done in 1855 and 1869. Over the years, points of reference had been moved, become lost or disintegrated.

Actual construction was started by grading crews on building sites on November 19, 1940. At that time there existed only preliminary surveys of the contours. Detailed plans and other data were still in preparation. The general plan of the camp layout was prepared and submitted to the Corps Area Commander, Lt. Col. Oliver Marston, for his approval about November 18, 1940.

The plan was to start where buildings were to be located and to construct temporary roads into these areas. After this, building construction was started. About 90 per cent of all construction materials was shipped by rail to San Miguel.

The contractors and subcontractors were handicapped by a lack of labor and by the fact that the laborers who were willing to work on this project required sufficient overtime pay to compensate them for having to live in an isolated area and for having to pay much more for board and lodging.

To induce men to stay on the job, or to come from the larger cities where there was plenty of work, a 58-hour work week (ten hours for five days and eight hours on Saturday) was implemented. Based on regular scales, here are some examples of the weekly pay: Foreman, $150; Carpenter, $75; Electrician, $105; Unskilled Laborer, $50; Machinist, $81; Lumber Carrier Driver, $87; Bulldozer Driver, $100; Tractor Driver, $84; Painter, $83; Plumber, $100; Truck Driver, $58 - $67, and Iron Worker, $81.

The added hours and increased earnings enabled the contractors to obtain needed labor to meet the schedules for the arriving troops.

The labor employed was entirely union, drawn from union locals which had, or claimed, jurisdiction. At the start of work, considerable difficulty was encountered adjusting wage scales because the Secretary of Labor's wage scale of November 2, 1940, did not entirely agree with local wage scales. These were adjusted satisfactorily by paying the higher scale in most cases.

Weather conditions at the start were good, but the rain started on December 16, 1940, and lasted through April of 1941. Rainfall recorded at the Nacimiento Ranch House hit a record of 39.90 inches. During this period, there were 64 days of steady rain.

Some roads were washed out or became unusable, and the waterlogged excavation work severely hampered progress. The costs on all outside activities were increased by at least 33 per cent, and for grading and utility work, probably 100 per cent. Start of work on permanent roads was delayed at least three weeks. In many places, four to six feet of mud had to be taken out and replaced with new soil.

With all this mud, equipment bogged down. Some of the older workers said they had never seen anything like this.

While working on the parade ground, a large "Cat" tractor was mired up to the top of its tracks. This led to the rumor that there is still a piece of equipment buried in the parade ground.

In an interview, Harley Davidson, a foreman for Morrison-Knudsen at that time, said that it took 14 pieces of equipment to get the tractor out, but they did remove it. And all through the project they did not lose one piece of equipment, he said.

The contractors wanted to see how fast they could construct a barracks building, and through prior planning, constructed one in less than three days.

In an interview, Edna Slaton of Paso Robles told how her husband, Edgar, started working at the camp: When told of a construction project that was to start near San Miguel, he, his brother, Charles, and a neighbor headed north and found the major contractors just moving on to the Nacimiento Ranch.

The fences had been cut and equipment was being moved in. The three found the foreman, a Mr. Shriver, and they were hired immediately as guards.

Apparently these men were the first local men to be hired for the

MUD CAUSED CONSTRUCTION DEATH

In the winter of 1940-41, it rained a total of 42 inches-plus in San Luis Obispo. To say that construction conditions were unspeakable is to put it mildly. A family we know of—father, mother, two small boys—came from Texas so that the father could work on Camp San Luis Obispo construction. He was tragically crushed and killed when the bulldozer he was handling in that muck overturned.

—*Thomas A. Hunt*

THE GENERAL PROVED QUITE GENEROUS

The general had a housing allowance of $125 a month, but they could only charge him $25. It worked out all right, however, because the general was both generous and inventive.

In early 1942, Dr. Harry and Nathalie Bryan Wolf were willing to rent their home on Capitol Hill in Paso Robles to help ease the housing shortage for military personnel. Their pleasant home included a croquet court and a vineyard.

Maj. Gen. Rene Hoyle, the commander of Camp Roberts, became the tenant. But he felt bad about the rental agreement, because the U.S. Office of Price Administration had frozen the rent on the house to a maximum of $25 a month.

While he couldn't exceed that figure, he could include this agreement: "I'll keep up the yard, and if anything happens to the house, I'll fix it."

Nathalie's daughter, Jackie Bode, said she remembers that the general had a new roof put on the house and had it painted inside and out, among other improvements.

The Wolfs learned how much of an Army man the general was when he told them that "the Army is a family affair" for him and his wife as, together, they had 119 relatives in the Army.

—*Stan Harth*

project. The pay at that time was $1,800 per year. Their guard duties were terminated in the middle of April of 1941 and transferred to the Military Police.

Edna Slaton said her husband told her that he saw people turned away from jobs. Some had spent their last dollar to get to the site, but when they arrived they were told they had to be union members to obtain employment. To join the union they would have to go to San Jose or Los Angeles as there were no hiring halls in the area. Some of these people had their families with them and were without money for gasoline or food. Some sold all their possessions to buy gasoline. This problem was later solved by establishing union offices in the area.

During the construction, the contractors used some 30,600 gallons of paint, 35,000,000 board feet of lumber, and 100 carloads of Sheetrock.

The project was completed five days before the July 15 estimated completion date. Construction costs totaled $16,330,155.76.

In his "Completion Report," Captain Smoody wrote:

"No amount of wages or compensation is sufficient reward for the energy put forth in spite of the most unfavorable working conditions through the period of peak construction.

"To illustrate but one point, carpenters found it necessary to carry lumber to their work-site through knee-deep mud, and on occasion would be stuck so badly that they would drop their load and would need assistance to be rescued from their predicament. The plumbers had to lay their lines in trenches soft with mud; the heavy equipment operators required as many as three tractors to pull them out of the soft spots; all this had to be done to meet troop arrival schedules.

"The extra wet climate brought on illness to a great many in the form of influenza, colds, pneumonia, etc.

"The living conditions (were) chaotic, shelter for some of the workman consisting of abandoned chicken houses; in short, it is inconceivable that people would willingly submit to such trials for the sole privilege of working on this project in return for the wages. Only a high order of patriotism and duty to their country is the answer.

"It is also gratifying to note that during the whole period of seven months, with a peak of nearly 8,000 men and two and a half million dollars worth of construction equipment, there were no fatal accidents and a very low injury rate."

The original orders assigning officers and men to Camp Roberts came in February of 1941. These stated that the personnel would proceed to Camp Nacimiento, for this was the facility's name prior to General Order No. 1 of January of 1941. That order named the new training station "Camp

Library staff members Kay Sickbert and Virginia Peterson participate in a gas mask drill at Camp Roberts. *Photo courtesy of Virginia Peterson.*

Roberts," after Corporal Harold D. Roberts, a Congressional Medal of Honor winner in World War I. Camp Roberts became the first United States Army installation to be named in honor of a non-commissioned officer.

In January of 1941 only about one-fifth of the facilities was ready for occupancy. Tents and shacks for the construction offices were almost as numerous as the facilities which had been prepared for the soldiers.

A discussion then arose over the destiny of the only tree on the parade ground. Many wagers were made as to the final disposition. Even plans for a formal funeral were suggested. When it was finally decided to leave the tree, grading and filling of the parade ground began.

The first troops, mostly one-year volunteers, arrived on March 15, 1941.The red letter day arrived for them when trucks deposited boxes of 1903 Springfield rifles that had been stored and sealed between 1918 and 1920. Each company was issued about 200 gallons of solvent to clean the weapons.

Training areas were selected primarily on the basis of where the ground was solid, and often the grass, poison oak and snakes had to be removed first. Quite often the poison oak won the battle for survival.

The large parade ground was finally paved, and spectators were able to watch the soldiers march. After the rains, the mud became fine dust that swirled when the winds increased during late afternoons. There also were many range fires that were probably started by training.

December 7, 1941, brought chaos to Camp Roberts and an immediate exodus of troops and officers. Troops were temporarily sent to increase the strength of other units stationed along the West Coast in preparation for an

The barracks at the camp were spartan. *Photo courtesy of Al Davis.*

expected invasion. Those troops who remained faced training alerts, air raid drills and blackouts. Soon, new recruits began to arrive by the thousands.

Graduates of Camp Roberts during World War II will recall the 17 weeks of intensive training; the 20-mile hikes with full field equipment; the "boom" of the 75mm cannon located at camp headquarters on "Mount Olympus," which announced reveille along with the bugle; the mock French village where trainees learned about booby traps and combat in cities, and the chatter of the .30 caliber machine guns on the ranges.

During the war Maj. Gen. Rene E. de Russey Hoyle, Commander of Camp Roberts, probably summed up what Camp Roberts was all about. He told a graduating class: "In this coming year, all or most of you will be sent where the war is...we have trained you the best we know...how you use that training is your responsibility...use it wisely, use it untiringly...use it violently, be a credit to yourself and to the Army."

WARTIME HUMOR

The Post commander called on 2nd Lt. Oliver A. Batcheller, who was an expert in horticulture, to cheer up the camp with trees, flowers and shrubs. Then he told the lieutenant that he thought that a sign was needed to show where Camp Roberts was. Lt. Batcheller, along with "yardbirds" from the post stockade, constructed a large sign some 100 feet tall that said "U.S. ARMY—CAMP ROBERTS."

It took several months to construct and, when completed, the Commander was proud of it. The sign was there for only three months when December 7th happened. Lt. Batcheller was again called to the Commander's office and was told, "What are you trying to do? Tell the Japanese where to bomb? Get that thing down." The lieutenant had to get the "yardbirds" again, this time to pull the sign down.   —*Al Davis*

A ROOKIE AT CAMP ROBERTS

by Private Ned Eller

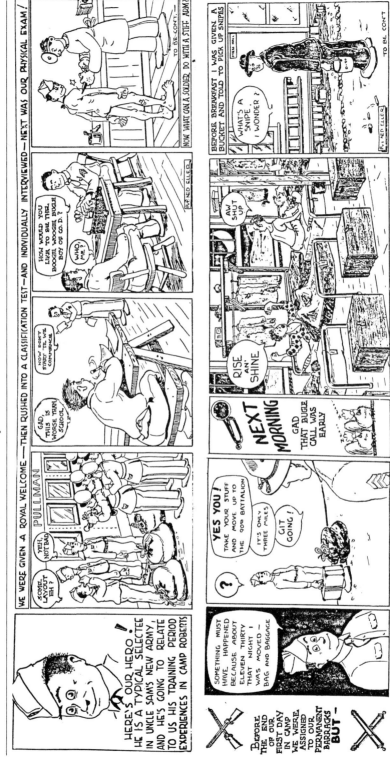

Lura Rawson

FIRST CAMP CONSIDERED TOO TOUGH FOR TROOPERS

In the early 1900s, Rancho Atascadero, smallest of the land grants along El Camino Real, was considered by the government as a potential site for what was termed "A School of War." This would be a permanent installation to train troops to serve in the islands and other possessions in the Pacific.

A provisional camp was set up in 1904 under the command of General Arthur MacArthur, father of General Douglas MacArthur of World War II and Korean War fame. The instructors included West Pointers and personnel seasoned in military campaigns.

The camp was described as being near Atascadero Creek about one-half mile south of the railroad. That would place it in the vicinity of the present day city administration building in Atascadero.

Black troops had been sent to the site earlier to set up the camp and get everything ready. The regular session was from August 13th to 28th. About 4,500 persons were involved in the daily operations. Represented

Vintage tents comprised temporary Camp Atascadero. *Photo courtesy of San Luis Obispo County Historical Museum.*

Bread baking during maneuvers at Camp Atascadero. *From a 1910 postcard.*

were the 1st, 2nd, 5th, 6th and 7th Regiments of the California Infantry as well as the U.S. troops who had arrived earlier. A complete hospital, capable of serving 100 patients, was made ready.

The temperature of the first day hit 110 degrees Fahrenheit. Maneuvers were limited to advance and deploy simulations in order to "break the men in easy" as they were not "seasoned." The ground was very rough and increased the hardships of marching. After deployment, the 1st Brigade was in a line of battle some five miles long. It advanced five miles. This "easy" exercise resulted in the death by heat exhaustion of one private in the 6th California, and about 30 others had to be taken to the hospital.

A variety of exercises was conducted each day with the "Blue" and "Brown" troops. The weather continued hot, and many more suffered from heat exhaustion. More than 500,000 rounds of blank ammunition were used. Some of the battle exercises were conducted in the rugged terrain of the hills.

At the end of the two weeks, an evaluation of the camp and exercises was conducted. It was the opinion of General MacArthur that a more suitable location could be found, one nearer the ocean and away from the extreme heat. (Just a few years later, Atascadero Ranch was advertised nationally as having a perfect climate.) The review also concluded that the terrain was too rough for new recruits.

However, the California National Guard continued to hold training camps there in alternate years, for Mrs. Mazie Adams, historian for the Atascadero Museum, has found records of encampments in 1904, 1908 and 1910 and believes one was held in 1906 and possibly in 1912.

This story first appeared in the North County edition of the San Luis Obispo County Telegram-Tribune.

Mark Hall-Patton

CAMPS PISMO AND EDNA FAILED TO ATTRACT ARMY

Camp San Luis Obispo is a well known part of our county's heritage, but what about Camp Pismo Beach, or Camp Edna?

In 1901, the United States Congress authorized the army to look at possible sites for new bases, and Pismo Beach and the Edna Valley were two of the sites considered.

The "Act to Increase the Efficiency of the Permanent Military Establishment of the United States," passed in February of 1901, authorized preliminary surveys of possible military base sites throughout the nation.

In the South County, many different tracts were offered for examination. On January 11, 1902, the army committee, accompanied by John Whicher, C.H. Phillips and "Mr. Moore" (perhaps Patrick Moore), looked over the Callender Ranch, described as four miles south of Arroyo Grande and consisting of 8,400 acres. The land was for sale by the County Bank of San Luis Obispo and was much smaller than the 20,000 acres the army wanted. However, the bank representatives noted on the map they submitted to the army that there was enough land for sale contiguous to the ranch to make the 20,000 acres quite feasible.

The property consisted of rolling hills of sandy soil covered with a heavy growth of sagebrush. It had practically no timber, and though it bordered Berros Creek, it was without running water. The area covered by the options held by the County Bank ran from Arroyo Grande Creek to Oso Flaco Lake and inland to the Pacific Coast Railway tracks.

This was not the only land offered to the army. Reginald Nuttall, a real estate agent in San Luis Obispo, represented a 30,000-acre tract that ran from Edna to the Abrum Hasbrouck property on Saucelito Creek. This land would have covered part of the Edna Valley, Corbett Canyon, Verde Canyon, the Upper Arroyo Grande, parts of the Corral de Piedra and the Santa Manuela Ranchos and Arroyo Grande.

In his letter to General Kobbe of the army, Nuttall said the property was served by both the local Pacific Coast Railway and the transcontinental Southern Pacific. He wrote that the land was well watered by year-round streams as well as artesian wells on the Steele Ranch. Nuttall estimated the total cost of obtaining the lands in this tract to be about $600,000.

Whether Nuttall had the permission of the various landowners to offer their land for sale is not altogether clear, but he did imply it when he noted that the lands of the Santa Manuela Rancho were in the hands of an administrator for minor children and would have to be condemned or sold by court order. No other land was listed as being a major problem to obtain.

In addition to these two major sites, smaller ranches and tracts were offered to the government. C.J. Russell offered 800 acres between Grover and Oceano that fronted on the beach and extended inland into the Arroyo Grande Valley. Russell also felt another 1,000-acre ranch adjacent to his could be purchased at the same price of between $40 and $50 per acre.

A tract along Pismo Beach was offered by Charles Ricketts. It consisted of 1,000 acres for which Ricketts wanted only $1. Adjoining properties were available for $10 to $20 per acre.

Land on the Carrisa Plains was offered by C.A. Beckwith, and many North County sites`also were proposed. It seemed that everyone with large land holdings wanted to get into the act of selling land to the army.

No South County sites were in the final consideration. While Nuttall's had been considered a good possibility, it had been submitted after the committee had been to the county to view the sites.

This story first appeared in the South County edition of the San Luis Obispo County Telegram-Tribune.

Troops on the march during the 1935 Nipomo war games. *Photo courtesy of San Luis Obispo County Historical Museum.*

Mark Hall-Patton

RED FORCES BATTLED BLUE DURING NIPOMO TRAINING

In 1935 two mighty opposing armies were poised to fight in southern San Luis Obispo County. The Red Forces, under the command of General Walter P. Story, were gathering in Los Angeles. The Blue Forces, under General Wallace A. Mason and headquartered in San Francisco, were sent to hold the southern boundary of their territory: the Santa Maria River.

This was the scenario for one of the largest field maneuvers held in California up to that time. It was a National Guard exercise involving thousands of troops from California, Nevada and Utah; it was the largest assembly of elements of the 40th Division since World War I.

While military exercises dating back to 1904 had been held in the North County and at Camp Merriam, which later became Camp San Luis Obispo, this was the largest ever held in South County, involving some 5,000 troops.

One aspect of the maneuvers noted by the newspapers of the day was the use of one and one-half ton trucks "similar to ones used in Civilian Conservation Corps camps," according to the *Arroyo Grande Herald-Recorder*. The overall transportation needs for the thousands of participants were to be met by 12 station wagons and 119 trucks. Part of the reason for the exercise was to train the motor transport detachments in the moving of entire regiments.

On July 7, troops began assembling at the "camp on the Morro road," as Camp San Luis was called in the articles in the *Herald-Recorder*. There was some question about the effect of the troops on the Nipomo Mesa. There were to be thousands of troops skirmishing back and forth on the Mesa for a week. This might cause quite a bit of damage to the agricultural lands they would be fighting over. The troops and their commanders had been warned to be careful. According to the *California Guardsman* of May of 1935: "Exceptional precautions will be necessary in the maneuver area to prevent damage to growing crops and other private property. No state or federal funds are available to pay damages and if any are caused by troops the cost thereof probably will have to be met from the organization funds or assessed against the persons responsible."

Other cautions noted for the troops were the existence of poison oak which was to be "carefully avoided by the susceptible" and the existence of rattlesnakes, though recent brush fires had reduced this hazard.

Ready to fire as war games raged. *Photo courtesy of San Luis Obispo County Historical Museum.*

The maneuvers lasted from July 14 to 19 and were judged to be a great success. The Blue Army dug in on the Mesa after a forced march (no horses or vehicles even for staff officers) from Camp San Luis by way of Edna. That it was foggy was considered a realistic detail of the exercise.

The Red Army surprised the Blues by marching to their staging area after an all night train ride which enabled them to get into position after only a relatively short walk, while the Blues had been hiking for two days. Other Red forces came from the San Joaquin Valley by way of Highway 166.

The night of Sunday, July 14, was very dark, with the fog obscuring the moon. The Reds moved into position and attacked at 15 minutes before dawn on Monday. A drive was made by the 185th Infantry to capture General Mason's headquarters in Los Berros. The defending 184th weren't even awake when the attack started and began falling back. But a successful counterattack by the 159th halted the drive.

The exercise went back and forth, with the Reds being declared the winners. The exploits of one soldier should be remembered. He was Private George Hayes of Company K, 160th Infantry, one of the Red troops. Pvt. Hayes almost upset the entire exercise by infiltrating enemy lines, obtaining classified information, being captured by the Blues and escaping. While making good his escape, he casually sauntered up to a high ranking Blue officer and asked directions. Thinking Hayes was on the Blue side, the officer told him how to get to the road, and Hayes reciprocated by stealing the officer's plans and reports and taking them to the Red forces.

All in all, it was quite a war.

This article first appeared in an issue of the South County edition of the San Luis Obispo County Telegram-Tribune.

Dan Krieger

PILOTS-TO-BE WALKED HANCOCK FIELD RAMP

M*en who hated marching avoided the infantry. The Army Air Corps might seem like a refuge from sore feet. But that wasn't the way things were at Hancock Field.*

In May of 1939, the Hancock College of Aeronautics in Santa Maria became part of our nation's preparation for war. It was one of 63 private flight schools nationwide which would eventually train some 200,000 pilots for America in World War II.

Allan G. Hancock may have envisioned this wartime role when he founded the College of Aeronautics in 1928. "Captain" Hancock acquired that title by earning the license necessary to master any sea-going vessel. But he didn't earn his livelihood as a sea captain.

Hancock was a visionary capitalist. He founded San Francisco's Hibernian Bank in 1909 and the Rancho La Brea Oil Company in 1910. He was a principal in the development of Hancock Park and Sherman Oaks and a founder of the Los Angeles Philharmonic Orchestra. He endowed galleries in the Los Angeles County Museum of Natural History and building clusters at the University of Southern California.

P.T. Stearmans in a row on Hancock Field. *Photo courtesy of Everett Blakely.*

Then he turned his attention to the Santa Maria Valley. He bought the standard-gauge Santa Maria Valley Railway from a failed English partnership. Santa Maria was by-passed by the Southern Pacific in 1900. Under Hancock's aegis, the SMVRR was able to continue providing a vital commercial link with the Southern Pacific's Coast Route at Guadalupe.

Hancock went on to develop ranching, chicken and egg farming and food processing industries in the valley.

In 1928, he established the College of Aeronautics. "Lucky" Lindbergh had completed his famous transatlantic solo flight the year before. Hancock wanted to train pilots and maintenance personnel for America's burgeoning commercial aircraft industry.

Up to that time, most of the new pilots were trained in the reckless tradition of the "barnstorming" veterans of the Great War. Hancock wanted to professionalize pilots in the same fashion that he himself had studied oceanography and navigation of the sea lanes.

The Great Depression curtailed the expansion of America's aircraft industry. The Hancock College of Aeronautics was only kept alive by generous subsidies from Captain Hancock, but it survived the depression.

In May of 1939, General Henry "Hap" Arnold, Chief of the Army Air Corps, summoned the proprietors of eight of the largest flight schools to Washington, D.C.

Arnold asked that they begin training pilots for the Air Corps. He told them that it would be months before Congress could pass the necessary funding bills. There was a chance that the schools' owners might never be compensated. But it was necessary if America was to survive the anticipated Nazi aerial assault.

Everett Blakeley was in his junior year at the University of Washington in Seattle that year. Hitler had annexed Austria and had invaded Czechoslovakia. Then came the blitzkrieg invasions of Poland, Norway, France, Belgium and the Netherlands. Blakeley shared General Arnold's opinion that it wouldn't be long before America was involved in a major air war. He signed up for pilot training.

In August of 1941 he received orders to report for primary pilot school training at Hancock Field. Here is how he recalled his arrival: "Upon arriving at Santa Maria, I was greeted by the rather impressive gate at Hancock Field which read 'Hancock College of Aeronautics.' Upon reaching the flight line, I saw a row of 13 Stearman Primary Flight Trainers at the end of the ramp. Little did I realize how well I would come to remember that stretch of ramp, not for the aircraft, but for the many weekends spent 'walking the ramp'.

"I was one of 57 aviation cadets drawn from various universities and

Cadet Blakeley, far right, confers with other pilots. *Photo courtesy of Everett Blakeley.*

The first pilot in his group to solo receives special honors. *Photo courtesy of Everett Blakeley.*

nine freshly-commissioned second lieutenants from West Point. Together, we comprised the Class of 42 C.

"The next three months were filled with an intense mixture of drill and discipline. We had classes in the morning and flight training in the afternoon.

"On weekends we had to clear the demerits that we had acquired during the week for infringements of rules. Some demerits were for trivial offenses such as being late for drill, clothes not being properly buttoned, or failure to eat a 'square meal' in proper West Point fashion. This was where you were expected to bring your soup spoon up at a precise right angle.

"Demerits resulted in long hours of stiffly marching a long straight line painted on the ramp. Since misery loves company, we made lasting friendships passing one another or while on breaks from our walk!

"Once, I was engrossed in practicing my instructions on a solo flight. I had gone some distance out over the bean fields and grazing hills of the valley. I returned at what I thought was precisely the prescribed time. I was fully satisfied with myself. I was greeted quite abruptly by my flight instructor who bellowed out, 'Gopher Blakeley, that will be eight hours of ramp time this weekend. You were exactly one hour late on return.'

"I had lost track of time. I had to pay the price by walking down 'memory lane.' I'm certain the punishment was well deserved since the base was about to send out a search flight for my Stearman trainer."

This article first appeared in the January 19, 1991, San Luis Obispo County Telegram-Tribune.

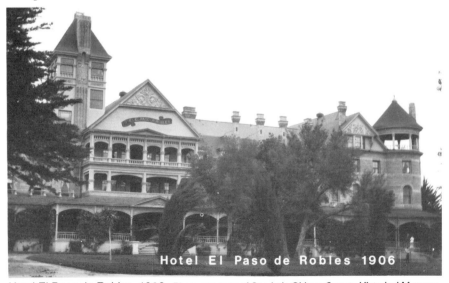

Hotel El Paso de Robles, 1906. *Photo courtesv of San Luis Obispo County Historical Museum.*

Al Davis, Camp Roberts Historian

PASO ROBLES LANDED FLYING FIELD IN '40

Years after the conclusion of World War II, residents of a new housing tract in the southeast quadrant of Paso Robles had a difficult time trying to plant shrubs and trees in their yards. That was because they were digging into the old runways and parking ramps of Sherwood Field, a facility to train women and men as civilian and military pilots.

Some of the airfield's structures remain. The building at 298 Sherwood Road was the steel hangar, while the officers' mess was the building at 320 Sherwood Road. The original hangar is used by the city as a fire station and utility building.

Initially developed in the late 1920s and early 1930s by T. A. Osborne, the airfield had two dirt strips for a few local owners of aircraft. Its first military use was in 1937 when it was part of the Fourth Army war games.

The 115th Squadron of the Air National Guard was one of the first occupants of Sherwood Field. *Photo courtesy of Al Musso.*

The airfield also was used by "barnstormers," itinerant pilots who would offer airplane rides for as little as one dollar, and it was a stopover for blimps traveling along the coast.

By February of 1940, the Paso Robles Chamber of Commerce, headed by Paul Turner, was exploring ways to improve the airfield. A $10,000 improvement program funded through the Civil Aeronautics Authority (CAA) was anticipated. But to be eligible for such a grant, the facility had to be owned or leased by a city, county or other political body.

Osborne offered to sell it to the city for $12,000 or to lease the runways for $500 per year for ten years. Paso Robles Mayor Liddle said that was too much. In a special session, the city council selected three possible alternate sites: 1) the present location of the Paso Robles airport; 2) a site off the highway to Shandon about one mile northeast of the city, and 3) a site on the Estrella Plain about four and one-half miles to the northeast.

The following week, the council set aside these alternatives and called for a special election on April 9, 1940, to decide whether to appropriate $9,000, payable in three installments, to acquire Sherwood Field. The measure passed by a margin of six to one.

On April 18, the CAA completed a field survey and recommended a light beam, radio signal tower and weather station and grading and weed removal. On July 18, the CAA called for reoiling the runways—they were 150 feet wide and 3,400 and 6,600 feet long—and the construction of a hangar, plus the removal of 35 trees.

These improvements were designed to prepare the facility for a proposed Civilian Pilots Training School. The deadline was August 1, 1940.

Plans were drawn for a 30-foot by 50-foot hangar that would cost $1,400. Woodchoppers, under the direction of J.H. Berry, cleared the trees. It appears the county provided some maintenance support.

By July 25, 36 student-pilots were enrolled, including one female, Betty Lyle, a daughter of Henry Lyle of Paso Robles. Ruth Candudy, Virginia Sanders and Mrs. Alan Loose joined on August 1, when the complement of 50 was reached.

The training course began with 72 hours of ground school conducted by H. R. Martinson, a professor of aeronautics at Cal Poly, and George Annis, an instructor at Hancock College of Aeronautics in Santa Maria. During this period, John Hibbard, Carl Von Stosten and Leslie Anderson achieved their instructor ratings.

On October 9, 1940, the city leased the facility to the War Department for one dollar a year. A week later, private planes were removed. On October 30, construction began on a $300,000 project for the Army. The L. E. Dixon Company, which was involved in the construction of Camp San Luis Obispo, was the contractor.

Hollywood starlets often visited Paso Robles through trips arranged by Johnny Monte of the 115th Air National Guard. *Photo courtesy of Al Musso.*

Much of the project consisted of water, sewage and drainage systems and underground electric and telephone lines. A large sewage plant was built at the southwest corner. A 50,000-gallon water reservoir was built. Over 5,000 feet of concrete drain tile and corrugated iron culverts lined both runways. Provision was made to double the facility's capacity if needed.

The 115th Observation Squadron of the California National Guard was the first unit to use the new airport. Dedicated in November of 1941, the facility was named in honor of Capt. George C. Sherwood, the first commanding officer of the 115th's Photo Section. He died in a civilian airplane crash in 1935.

The 115th's 38 officer-pilots and 159 enlisted men were primarily from the Los Angeles area. The unit was attached to the 40th Division, which was at Camp San Luis Obispo. The personnel lived in tent shelters, but the two mess halls were finished in redwood paneling with white pine and buff-colored wallboard—quite a departure from the standard design. The shower buildings and toilets also were permanent structures, and the new hangar was of steel.

Early in February of 1941, the government appropriated an additional $254,346 for a new east-west runway of some 4,200 feet, and Paso Robles purchased 20 more acres for this. The new runway could accommodate any type of land plane in use in 1941. All the runways were hard-surfaced and had concrete aprons.

Sherwood Field was in use throughout World War II.

This story is a condensation of a much more detailed account.

Dan Krieger

"HOLLYWOOD GANG" FILMED, "FOUGHT" IN AIR OVER COUNTY

Just two months before Japan attacked Pearl Harbor, Paso Robles witnessed a Great Train Robbery. It was staged by Al Musso and his Hollywood Gang.

Neither the stylish *Daylight* nor the midnight *Lark* was stopped along the Southern Pacific's Coast Route. The heist took place on the downtown streets of Paso Robles. The perpetrators, all members of the Army Air Corp's 115th Observation and Reconnaissance Squadron, were awarded the First Place Trophy in the Pioneer Day Parade on October 12, 1941.

Al Musso, now a very active resident of Cayucos, had his first encounter with the Central Coast in 1941, when he enlisted in the Air National Guard.

Al was working at a night job in the advertising department of Paramount Studios. He decided to take some time off and visit the World's Fair on San Francisco's Treasure Island. While staying in the city, Al received a telegram from his draft board. He had a Number 2 Selective Service number. That meant that he would be drafted within a few weeks.

America wasn't in the European war, but it seemed like we'd be going "Over There" real soon. Like so many American boys, Al recalled the literal slaughter of infantry troops along France's Western Front during the First World War. Al dreaded being drafted into the infantry. So he joined the 115th.

The 115th was a unit of the Air National Guard. Formed during the 1920s, it was based on a small airfield in Los Angeles' Griffith Park. Its roster included many men who, like Al, were employees of the big Hollywood studios. There were 21 officers and 110 enlisted men in the outfit.

Taking off from the short airstrip near Griffith Park's Traveltown, the 115th would take aerial photographs of the diverse terrain, industrial and transportation resources of the Los Angeles basin. Many of the photography techniques which increased the accuracy of bombing later in the war were developed by the 115th.

On March 3, 1941, the 115th was transferred to Paso Robles' Sherwood Field. This was before Pearl Harbor, but the men knew that they were leaving Hollywood for the duration.

Members of the Army Air Corp's 115th Observation and Reconnaissance Squadron. *Photo courtesy of Al Musso.*

Members of the 115th at rest. *Photo courtesy of Al Musso.*

Al Musso, far right, served as conductor on the 115th's "train" entered in Paso Robles' Pioneer Days Parade. *Photo courtesy of Al Musso.*

The 115th's flight surgeon, Maj. Reynolds D. Smith, was the house physician at Los Angeles' famed Biltmore Hotel. He convinced the Biltmore's chef to join the unit so that meals would be up to snuff. Maj. Smith later became Chief Flight Surgeon for the Fifth Air Force.

This was a class act in airmen's gear. The men made the best of their circumstances. When they arrived at the field southeast of downtown Paso Robles, the airmen learned that the eight-man tents had to be moved. These were on frames with heavy wooden floor boards. Al says, "I know now how the Egyptians made the pyramids. The officers put 20 men on each of the four sides of the tent platform. Then the 80 men would lift the tent into position."

The 115th would sometimes be called to flour bomb troops involved in the war games at Camp Roberts. Al would sit in the rear seat filling dozens of brown lunch bags with two pounds of flour. Then they would dive bomb the Red Army or the Blue Army as requested by the commandant at Camp Roberts.

The men on the ground hated the flyers. If any flour got on a soldier, he was counted as a casualty in the war games. No doubt the noncoms penalized such victims with extra KP.

The trainees at Camp Roberts also disliked the 115th because the flyboys got so much off-duty leave to go into Paso Robles. The men at

Roberts were restricted to the camp much of the time.

Once Al was ordered to tow a target on a 1,500-foot cable off what is now Montaña de Oro. Men on the cliffs from Camps San Luis Obispo and Roberts would fire at the target with Browning Automatic Rifles. The bullets were painted so that hits could be attributed to individual soldiers. When Al's aircraft landed, one of the ground crew pointed to a number of colored holes in the rudder of the O-47. Al figured that not even a bad shot could have been 1,500 feet off.

Inter-service rivalries aside, life at Sherwood Field was good. Johnny Monte, a still photographer from Warner Brothers, would arrange for movie starlets to come up for the weekend.

The men of the 115th got to know and love Paso Robles. They formed a baseball team composed of their own men. Then Johnny Monte formed a team of local girls. He requested ten baseball bats, probably from Warner Brothers. The studio sent 100 by mistake. The surplus was used for souvenirs and fuel for a barbecue.

They designed a very special entry for the Pioneer Day parade in October. The men constructed a Hollywood set train that employed a flight line tug to pull a locomotive with three flat cars made up as passenger cars.

The aircrews dressed up as cowboys and Indians and staged The Great Train Robbery along with Indians pursuing the train.

The fellows stationed at Paso Robles' Sherwood Field enjoyed first class entertainment. *Photo courtesy of Al Musso.*

This is a BC-1A of the type from which Al Musso almost fell 2,500 feet without a parachute. *Photo courtesy of Al Musso.*

In the last days of an America still at peace in that fall of 1941, the men of the 115th had made themselves part of the Paso Robles community. It's appropriate that the lone hangar of Sherwood Field still sits nestled among newly built suburban homes and a shopping center along Paso Robles' Airport Drive.

Six days after Pearl Harbor, the 115th was reassigned to an anti-submarine detail based at Morrow Field (now Norton AFB) in San Bernardino County.

One day, Al was flying as the photographer in a BC-1A, a single-winged monoplane. He unstrapped his parachute as the aircraft was flying over a convoy of trucks taking Japanese-Americans from the San Pedro area to the temporary relocation camp at Santa Anita racetrack.

Just over Pasadena, Al stood up in the open observer's cockpit. He told the pilot not to bank until he gave instructions. For a few seconds, Al was standing while holding a massive aerial camera, with his upper torso out of the fuselage. He was busy adjusting the machine-gun-gripped camera's controls. The pilot banked unexpectedly. Al began to fall out of the aircraft. Fortunately, the weight of the camera and the force of the prop wash propelled him fully back into the aircraft, scrunching Al behind his seat so hard that the pilot couldn't see him. The shaken pilot, convinced that Al had fallen 2,500 feet to his death, was relieved when Al re-emerged!

The unit was integrated into the Army Air Corps and the men were sent to outposts from New Guinea to England, West Africa and the Mediterranean. But that's a story for other Fiftieth Anniversaries.

Cliff Nordstrom

CAMP SLO CARPENTER
RECALLS RAIN, MUD

Rain and cold waged war with us when we built Camp San Luis Obispo, so much so that we even had to invent ways to enable us to hold our tools.

I came to the camp in 1941 with a friend, Ross Becker. Ross became a carpenter foreman, and I was given a carpenter's job building wooden floors for tent hutments.

What I remember most is that it never seemed to quit raining. But we worked through it.

The lumber for these tent floors was cut to length in a mill set up adjacent to where we assembled them. We made jigs to assemble the 2x4-inch framing and floor joists, then we nailed 1x4-inch tongue-and-groove flooring to them. When we completed a 16x16-foot floor, we stockpiled it to be picked up later and taken to be set up with the tent.

We used what is called a rigging axe—a tool used those days in the oil fields—rather than a carpenter's hammer. Because the weather was so wet

Workmen battled record wet weather to build Camp San Luis. *Photo Courtesy of San Luis Obispo County Historical Museum.*

and cold, we would rub paraffin on the axe handle. Then the heat from our hands would melt the paraffin and form grips that made it easier for us to hold onto the axes.

Among our diversions was playing a form of poker based on the numbers on our paychecks. I recall a time when a dispute arose over who had won and one of the workers ended up with a broken jaw.

We stayed in a tent area erected for construction workers and ate in a mess hall. Once on my way to eat, I stepped out of my tent into a driving rain, missed the steps and ended up knee-deep in mud.

Some time later we moved to Pismo Beach and stayed in the Restwell Motel. We commuted to the camp by car pool, and the trips were very slow because of the narrow roads and the heavy traffic caused by so many persons who worked there.

THE LAST CIVILIANS TO LEAVE THAT DAY

Avice and Alice Wilkinson with Pfc. Paul Leachman. Photo courtesy of Alice and Avice Wilkinson.

Alice and Avice Wilkinson were equally shocked.

They were USO volunteers attending a Sunday open house at Camp San Luis.

The identical twin sisters had just finished lunch in one of the camp's mess halls when the news of the attack on Pearl Harbor came blaring over the camp's loudspeaker system. The Army post went on immediate alert.

Alice had been dating Pfc. Paul Leachman, who that day had given a demonstration on how to field strip a .50-caliber heavy machine gun.

Avice broke down in tears. She was scheduled to leave by bus on Dec. 12 for Wichita Falls, Texas, where she was going to marry Lt. Isaac E. Boniface, who was attending a flight mechanics school there.

Because the camp was on alert, the soldiers who had brought the sisters there were unable to take them home. So they had to take a taxi. And they were the last civilian visitors to get off the post that day.

—Stan Harth

Phil Amborn

YOUNG OFFICER CRITICIZED FIRST LADY'S COLOR CHOICE

Eleanor Roosevelt selected the colors in which the barracks at Camp Roberts and Camp San Luis Obispo were painted. I know, because I had other ideas that conflicted with the First Lady's choices.

As a first lieutenant, I was assigned to the office of Colonel Edward M. George, who was in charge of nearly all Army construction on the West Coast in early 1941.

The heavy rains and mud of the winter of 1940-41 slowed the construction of both camps, and the press began to print articles about the adverse conditions under which the soldiers were serving. The drab appearance of the unpainted buildings came in for criticism, although the articles failed to suggest how to paint wet buildings.

When the rains let up and the weather warmed, I was sent to the Los Angeles factory of the paint firm which was the low bidder to expedite paint shipments to the camps. I impressed upon the firm's managers that they should implement extra shifts until paint was arriving at the camps faster than it could be applied.

Upon my return to the office, and with all the brashness of a young lieutenant, I pointed out to my superiors that the lead and zinc pigments called for in the contract were using metals that were in short supply and, furthermore, that earth colors would be better and would also have some camouflage value.

I was told to forget it because Mrs. Roosevelt had picked out the cream color for the structures and the green for the roofs. She thought a bright, homey appearance would be of great benefit to the morale of our servicemen.

WARTIME HUMOR

Don McMillan's Political Platform re: National Defense...

The "Sage of Shandon" took a gentle swipe at political rhetoric with his advocacy of "more hostesses and fewer 15-mile hikes," "elimination of K.P. (Kitchen Police) and reveille" and deferment of those with "flat pocketbooks instead of those with flat feet."

—Millin' Around with McMillan
Telegram-Tribune, August 2, 1941

Governor Gave Himself An Honor

Camp San Luis Obispo didn't always bear that name.

For a short period, its name was changed to Camp Merriam.

And that name was conferred by a California governor to honor himself. He was Frank Merriam. In 1934, he defeated Upton Sinclair, an author and socialist, for the governorship, and then proceeded to wage battle against what he perceived to be subversive left-wingers.

To underscore what he believed to be the importance of that campaign and the prominence of his role in it, he renamed the California National Guard camp. Camp San Luis Obispo, the original name conferred on the facility in the 1920s, was out; Camp Merriam was in.

But only for a short time, for the federal government had other criteria for the naming of its facilities, and when it took over the military installation and began a sweeping expansion of it, the name Camp San Luis Obispo was back.

Another politician became involved with the camp in 1941. He was a U.S. Senator from Missouri who headed a Senate committee investigating national defense projects. He was Harry S Truman, the future president, and Camp San Luis was one of nine such facilities throughout the nation which came under attack by his committee for alleged extravagance.

A World War I captain of artillery, Truman looked at the $17,000,000 which the government had spent on expanding and improving the camp and, through his committee, tabbed that cost "unduly and unnecessarily high."

Certainly the record rainfall that winter of 1940-41 (36 inches by the end of March) was a factor in the overall cost. So, too, was the construction of Rinconada Dam to develop a reservoir to supply water to the troops. This later became Lake Santa Margarita. Then there were major improvements to Highway 1 and the construction of a railroad spur line to transport materials to the camp.

Hutments, with wood floors and sides and canvas tops, replaced tents, and recreation and entertainment facilities were built. In fact, Senator Truman might have been particularly incensed if he had learned that the camp added an ornate amphitheater with a seating capacity of 12,000 and such innovations as a "curtain" of water that sprayed upward to obscure the audience's view of the stage during scene changes.

—Stan Harth

Harold Gill

PAPERBOY TOILED AS CAMP SAN LUIS GREW

In 1940, when I was 12 years old, my older brother, Jack, and I sold out-of-town newspapers in San Luis Obispo by shouting the headlines on street corners and at train and bus depots.

Our younger brothers, Jim and Howard, would help us, and together we would earn about $3.75 each Sunday.

Then came the $17,000,000 project which turned Camp Merriam, a National Guard training post, into Camp San Luis Obispo between the fall of 1940 and the summer of 1941. Jack and I began earning about $50 a month as newsboys at a time when buck privates in the Army were earning $21 a month.

The camp still was under construction when the 40th Infantry Division arrived to find a sea of mud produced by one of the wettest winters on record. The troops were camped in muddy tents in muddy fields. What's more, most of the soldiers drilled with broomsticks rather than rifles, and the few trucks that the division had bore cardboard signs that identified them as "Tank" or "Command Car" or whatever role the maneuvers called for. It wasn't much of an army, but the soldiers didn't care, for they expected to go home after their one year of duty was completed.

During winter, I sold the *San Francisco Call-Bulletin.* Each paperboy was assigned a regiment and had to compete with boys who were trying to sell other newspapers. I went through my regiment every afternoon after school and was able to sell about 100 papers daily. Since I made two cents on each nickel paper I sold, I could average about $2 a day. But it usually took extraordinary effort to get a soldier to part with a nickel because of the low pay. So, if sales were slow, we would make up headlines like "Lana Turner Marries Soldier" or "Rita Hayworth Swims Nude In Fountain." That usually got the soldiers out of their tents.

As winter turned into spring, Camp San Luis was nearing completion, and the soldiers moved into the newly erected hutments. These wooden platforms with tent tops held six soldiers each. The hutments were laid out in a company grid, with a mess hall at one end and a latrine at the other. Roads were paved, and PXes (Post Exchanges) and recreation buildings were constructed.

We never sold all of our newspapers, even if we could. For they were

Paperboy Harold Gill was senior class president at San Luis Obispo Senior High School. *Photo courtesy of Tiger Tales.*

our currency of exchange. A newspaper presented to a mess sergeant produced a free dinner. When we hitchhiked, we stuck out the thumb of one hand and in the other hand we held out a newspaper. And the bags in which we carried our newspapers served as our uniform, enabling us to go wherever we pleased. Almost always the first jeep, truck, command car or tank that came by would stop for us.

Once I got a ride with a general in his big, open command car. I sat in the back with the general who was chewing on a cigar. To my surprise, he accepted the newspaper I offered him without paying me for it. When I saw another paperboy up ahead who was hitchhiking, I told the driver to keep going, and he did. As we passed the boy, I stood up and saluted. Then I realized it was Jack, so we stopped.

If a USO show was scheduled, we hitchhiked to the division auditorium. I learned to go around to the back where the buses for the performers were. I sold newspapers to entertainers Bob Hope, Red Skelton and Skinny Ennis, the band leader. While she never bought a newspaper from me, I fondly remember having the opportunity to watch Frances Langford. After I sold newspapers to the performers, I would go to the back door of the auditorium and give one to the guard. He would let me in so that I could stake out seats for the other paperboys.

But most nights we paperboys would meet at a central recreation hall where we would shoot pool while awaiting our ride back to town. We made a little money that way, too. For most of the soldiers weren't too good at pool but thought they could beat 12- and 13-year-old kids. On some summer evenings, we would run the obstacle course just for fun.

It was during the summer of 1941 that Jack and I switched to the *San Francisco Chronicle*, a morning newspaper. This meant that we had to get up at 4:30 o'clock in the morning to meet the train at 5 o'clock and get the newspapers. But the change was worth it, for I was assigned to the 185th Regiment, the first one we passed on entering the camp, and Jack got the hospital which was the second stop.

Since we got to the camp before the soldiers were up and about, I had to devise a new system to sell my newspapers: I put them in each mess hall with a cereal bowl beside them so the soldiers had some place to put their nickels or make change, and I gave each mess sergeant a free newspaper in exchange for watching out for that bowl of money. After awhile I knew how many readers there were in each company and how to distribute the newspapers accordingly. At the last mess hall, I gave a newspaper to the head cook in exchange for breakfast, usually steak and eggs. Then I would retrace my route, picking up the money and any newspapers that were left. To sell the remainder, I would walk through the regiment, shouting headlines that were real or made up.

Except for the officers' mess hall, the system worked wonderfully well. I was selling up to 200 newspapers each morning, seven days a week. By 7 o'clock in the morning, most of us had finished and hitchhiked to a recreation hall to play pool. We were able to get into the locked hall because the sergeant in charge had shown us where he hid the key. We always left a newspaper on his desk, of course.

I never had trouble being paid for my newspapers at the enlisted men's mess halls. Sometimes I would get an IOU, but it would always be redeemed on pay day, usually with substantial new "interest."

But the officers' mess hall was a different matter: the newspapers would be taken without being paid for, and the mess sergeants couldn't do much about it. One time, though, the commanding general of the division was eating breakfast at the officers' mess hall of my regiment. He hadn't noticed where I had placed my newspapers, and when I came in to collect my money—I had been shorted, as usual—he called me over to buy a newspaper. Then when he asked me how things were going, I told him. He stood up and loudly said some very pointed things to the assembled officers. He also ordered the mess sergeant to keep an eye on my newspapers and report to him about anyone who failed to pay. I was embarrassed, but it solved my problem.

There was one problem that was not solved and has not been to this day: I don't come awake easily. So after we switched to selling a morning newspaper, Jack usually had the task of getting me up in those chilly, predawn hours while the rest of the family slept.

We would grab a quart of milk from the refrigerator as we left the house. I would be wearing the bags I carried my newspapers in and an Army hat that was adorned with my regiment's insignia. We would go in the darkness directly to a bakery where we would each plunk down a nickel on the counter and receive a crushed fruit pie that was about six inches in diameter and that had been rejected by the baker for some imperfection. Of course, the people in the bakery knew us, but there seldom was any talk, for we weren't awake and they weren't in the mood at that early hour.

Most of the other paperboys followed the same routine. After making our purchases at the bakery, we would walk up to the railroad station and climb into the old, wood-paneled station wagon of our supervisor, Ed Kelly. Silently we would drink our milk, passing around the bottle, and eat our pies. Ed usually would be in the station master's office. By the time we got our newspapers and had ridden to camp, even I was reasonably awake. And by 8 o'clock, when Ed collected us to drive us back to town and school, I was ready for the day.

During the middle of the fall of 1941, mother consented to let Jim sell newspapers at the camp if Jack and I watched out for him. She had no idea what a paperboy's life there was really like. At the age of 10, Jim probably was the youngest paperboy there. He couldn't carry all of his newspapers in one load, so he had to make two trips. And when the bags were empty, they tended to drag on the ground because he was so short.

I gave Jim the 185th Regiment and moved to one of the regiments at the other end of the camp. Jim was a popular paperboy, and he often would invite soldiers to our home.

One day in December of 1941, the entire Gill family was invited to have Sunday lunch in one of the mess halls with a number of the soldiers from various companies whom he had invited to our home at one time or another. The cook even baked a cake for our mother.

Jack and I sold our newspapers, then hitchhiked over to the mess hall at Jim's regiment where the lunch was to be held. We waited there for Dad, Mom, Frances and Howard. It was a warm and beautiful day. A creek ran along the edge of the regimental area, and some soldiers had driven their trucks into a shallow bend of it so they could wash them. It was a relaxed and pleasant scene.

So was the lunch until a sergeant came in and said Pearl Harbor had been bombed. None of us was sure where Pearl Harbor was. We kept on eating our meal. Then an officer came in and said all leaves and passes had been canceled and all civilians had to leave the base. We then knew it was serious but we didn't realize just then how historic that day was. When our car topped the hill north of San Luis Obispo, we could hear the horn at the firehouse blasting away. Dad stopped the car, got out, listened and said, "We're at war."

Monday, December 8th, was a cloudy and damp day. It was a Holy Day at Mission School, so there were no classes. The train with the newspapers didn't arrive on time. So the non-Catholic paperboys went on to school, but we stayed at the depot. When the train finally arrived, we loaded the newspapers into Ed's truck and started for the camp. But Ed had a difficult time getting across Highway 101, for troop convoys from Fort Ord

In recreation rooms like this, 12-year-old Harold Gill supplemented his income from selling newspapers. *Photo courtesy of San Luis Obispo County Historical Museum.*

formed a seemingly endless stream along the highway. People lined the streets to watch the trucks roll by, but I don't remember that there was any cheering. Instead I recall that their faces reflected the dark and somber mood of the weather.

We could have sold all of our newspapers right there, but we didn't try. We went on to the camp. When I got to my regiment, the soldiers were in trucks that were ready to leave for the defense of Los Angeles. I sold all of my some 300 newspapers in just a few minutes.

Then I worked harder than I have ever worked. For the soldiers in the last trucks of the convoy began to give me five and ten dollar bills and asked me to run to the PX and buy candy bars for them. The nearest PX was about a half mile away. I ran there and bought $40 to $50 worth of candy and cookies, then ran back to the trucks.

By then, the engines of the trucks were running and the fumes and noise were almost overwhelming. But I could hear the soldiers in the trucks further up the line calling to me. They wanted the same thing, and I repeated the process, buying whole boxes of candy and cookies for them.

I was the only customer at the PX, and I told the sales clerk to stack up all the edibles on the counter because I would be back. I carried the foodstuff in my newspaper bags and ran as hard as I could. By about the fifth trip, I had purchased all the candy and cookies and was taking potato chips and ice cream bars and whatever else there was to eat. Each time I had to run further as I worked my way up the line of trucks.

On my last trip, the trucks were moving slowly forward. I ran to get to the first truck in line and threw food in each of the trucks as they passed. I have no idea if this was fair, but nobody complained.

The soldiers yelled and waved and thanked me as their trucks passed by where I stood drenched in sweat, with wobbly legs and gasping for breath.

I was the only one around to see them off.

After the trucks had gone beyond my sight, I sat on the edge of the now empty road, alone in the quiet.

Then, as I recall very well, I cried for awhile.

The first two permanent buildings at Camp San Luis Obispo were the Paymaster's Office (top) and the Post Office (bottom). *Photos courtesy of San Luis Obispo County Historical Museum.*

Elliot Curry

LAST HORSEBACK "BATTLE" WAGED ON SAN LUIS RANGE

In all the excitement and confusion that followed the attack on Pearl Harbor, not many San Luis Obispo people were aware that one of the few horse cavalry actions of World War II was taking place in the county.

One who remembers it very well, however, is A.E. "Tony" Ruda, who was guide and scout for the expedition, along with his brother, Joe Ruda.

In those frantic December days of 1941, there was a general fear and suspicion that the Japanese might have saboteurs or spies along the coast, ready to direct an attack on California.

One of the most likely spots for an enemy hideout appeared to be the San Luis Mountain range, which rises between Los Osos Valley and the Point Buchon-Diablo Canyon shoreline.

The Army moved quickly to find out what, if anything, was going on in the canyons and caves which indent these mountains, crossed only by cattle trails. Six hundred cavalrymen and their horses were dispatched here from Fort Ord to make a sweep of the entire area. The cavalry camped near the mouth of Islay Creek, near what is now the entrance to Montaña de Oro State Park.

Tony and Joe Ruda joined them there, and the party was split into two units of 300 horsemen each as they prepared for the five-day ride. The Ruda family had lived in these mountains for three generations and nobody knew the terrain better.

The cavalrymen were mostly young recruits from the plains of Ohio, and the horses had been doing maneuvers along the sandy beaches of Monterey County. Neither riders nor horses were ready for the oak and chaparral-covered mountains and deep-cut canyons which rise abruptly from the ocean.

Rounding a rocky promontory one day, where soil was thin, Tony Ruda advised the officers to have the men keep their feet out of the stirrups so they could fall free in case their horses slipped. They complied with some misgivings, but a short time later when they looked back at the line of march, nine horses were down.

One rider had decided to keep his feet in the stirrups. He was taken back to camp with a broken leg—the only casualty of the "engagement."

The men were carrying Army rations, and in true GI fashion the first day out, some tossed their food away as unfit for their taste. Tony quietly gathered the rations up and carried them in a sack on his saddle. Before the day's riding was over, the fussy appetites were cured and the men were retrieving their discarded food.

Every cave and every canyon was combed by the horsemen. What a surprise it would be to any who might return today and see Diablo Canyon.

As for Japanese spies or secret radio stations, there was not a sign. In one deserted house, some letters in Japanese were found, but they had no bearing on the war.

For the cavalrymen, it was their last horseback "battle." Upon their return to Ford Ord, they were mechanized.

This story originally appeared in the December 7, 1968 issue of the Telegram-Tribune.

WARTIME HUMOR

German Flyer (at gates of Heaven): "We'd like to come in."
St. Peter: "How many are there in your group?"
Flyer: "Forty."
St. Peter: "Sorry, only four of you can enter."
Flyer: "Why?"
St. Peter: "That's all Goebbels said were shot down."
—*SHOT 'N SHELL*
May 6, 1942

"Hey, you act as though you own the place," said the ruler of Hades as Hitler walked in.
"I do," replied Schnicklegrubber (sic), "The Yanks just gave it to me."
—*SHOT 'N SHELL*
May 20, 1942

Soldier's Lament: "I'm sure she's sincere, but why are her letters mimeographed?"
—*SHOT 'N SHELL*
April 8, 1942

Question: "Do you neck with the lights on or off?"
Answer: "Yes."
—*SHOT 'N SHELL*
May 6, 1942

Part 2

FAR FROM OUR SHORES

Dr. Maria Barrows, as a teenager, was forced to flee from Austria. *Photo courtesy of Dr. Maria Barrows.*

Marion Wolff lived in Vienna during Hitler's *Anschluss*. She escaped via a "children's transport" to England where she was reunited with her mother nine months later. *Photo courtesy of Paul Wolff.*

The Editors

HITLER'S HORRORS RECALLED BY FIVE LOCAL RESIDENTS

There are residents of San Luis Obispo who well remember the specter that was Nazi Germany in the 1930s and who understand the importance of the county's contribution to the fight for freedom in World War II.

They include Henry and Lise Marx, who awoke one morning while on their honeymoon in 1934 to find swastikas unfurled in Venice; Paul and Marion Wolff, who experienced the horrors signaled by *Kristallnacht*, and Dr. Maria Barrows, whose native Austria was overrun by German troops in 1938.

The episode of the Nazi flags was reported by Dorie Bentley in the *San Luis Obispo County Telegram-Tribune* of April 21, 1990, this way:

Lise Marx has vivid memories of her honeymoon in 1934. "We woke up in Venice and looked out the window. Swastikas were all over." The symbols of Nazi Germany and anti-Semitism marked a historic meeting between Hitler and Mussolini.

Lise and her future husband, Henry Marx, met in 1929 at a costume ball. "She was the cutest little Indian squaw, and I was the ugliest ratcatcher in Hamelin," Henry said.

"On June 3, 1934, we were married in Stuttgart in the presence of relatives and friends in the same synagogue Henry had become bar mitzvah 14 years earlier—and which was burned to the ground on *Kristallnacht* on November 9, 1938," Lise said.

The newlyweds left Berlin behind in 1937 to come to the United States.

Kristallnacht, "The Night of Broken Glass," is often regarded as the start of the Holocaust. Thousands of Jewish shops in German cities and towns were broken into; more than 10,000 Jewish homes were destroyed, and more than 30,000 Jews were arrested and sent to concentration camps.

In an interview with Dan Krieger, Paul Wolff recalled that night when men came at 2 o'clock to pound on the door of his home in Hamburg: "I was nine, but I clearly remember Mom, in her housecoat, arguing with those Nazis. She showed them the papers and numerous medals, including the Iron Cross, which had been awarded to Dad during the last war. The

Nazis weren't interested in the medals or prior service to Germany. They wanted to know Dad's whereabouts."

As there had been no attempt to keep that a secret, Paul's mother gave them the information. His father was arrested that night and held for nine days.

Marion Wolff's mother was German and her father was an Austrian. She was born in Berlin in 1930. Because of what was happening to Jews in Germany, her father took the family to Vienna in Austria, where he died in 1937. The following March, Hitler launched his *Anschluss*, the forced unification of Austria with Nazi Germany.

In remembering that, Marion painted this scene: "Black boots marching; old men on their hands and knees in front of the temple scrubbing the streets;.black boots kicking; swastikas all over the place; Jewish shops and homes sealed up; coming home from school and being surrounded by larger children who taunted me, called me *saujude* (Jewish swine)."

At the time of *Kristallnacht*, Marion was told that she no longer could stay in school. "My teacher looked so helpless as she said goodbye," she said.

Dr. Barrows also was in Vienna during the *Anschluss* on March 12 and 13 of 1938. She was 12 years old. Her recollection includes this: "Many private schools, including the convent school I attended, were closed; textbooks were substituted. Austrian history was no longer a subject in the schools that remained open.

"Within one week, my father's medical practice and his personal car were confiscated, and he fled to England. The reason for this confiscation was that my father was of Jewish background, although his father had been a convert to Catholicism, and his mother was not a practicing Jew. I was raised a Catholic.

"Nevertheless, according to the (Nazi) law of racial supremacy, our family was part Jewish and had to relinquish many rights. I learned the meaning of the word *mischling*, which was the term for children of mixed marriages, and it had a despicable connotation. However, I was not required to wear the Star of David, which identified persons brought up as Jews living under the Nazis. If they left their homes, they had to wear the Star of David."

While Lise and Henry Marx were able to escape the Holocaust, 18 of their relatives became its victims. After living in New York City and Denver, the couple moved to San Luis Obispo in 1989 to be near their son, Steven, a professor of English literature at Cal Poly, and his family.

Marion Wolff also was able to escape, because she was sent on a "children's transport" to England. This is how she recalled her departure from the Vienna train station: "I was one of the youngest children there. I put on a brave front, as did my mother. One of the last things she gave me was a pair of hand-knitted knee socks. I clutched them to my body as the train left."

She and her mother were reunited nine months later in England, but she said most of the children never saw their parents again.

Because they had a relative in New York City who would sponsor their entry into the United States, Paul Wolff's family was able to leave Hamburg by ship in the spring of 1939. After 31 days at sea, their ship sailed under the Golden Gate, which was new and painted gold.

Paul and Marion met in San Francisco in 1960. Today he is a professor of architecture at Cal Poly.

It wasn't until April of 1940 that Dr. Barrows was able to escape. She remembered it this way: "We had just about given up hope that I would be able to leave. I was one of four *mischling*, all 15-year-olds, who were chosen by a Quaker organization doing relief work in Vienna. They would sponsor us for emigration to the United States. Two of us had regular passports. The other two had been raised as Jews and had 'J' prominently stamped on their passports.

"I was very excited and, at long last, found the courage to tell my schoolmates in an unaccredited, private, college-preparatory school that I was going to leave. They were very fearful for me. They said, 'You should think twice about going to America! That's where all the gangsters are!'

"On April 13, shortly before Italy was drawn into the war, we left Vienna by train to take an Italian ship from Genoa to New York City."

Since he was an Austrian, Dr. Barrows' father had been interned as an enemy alien on the Isle of Man, but as a doctor, he worked in the refugee camps that were organized by the British.

"Since I had been raised Catholic," Dr. Barrows continued, "the Quakers put me under the care of Catholic Social Services in New York. I was able to contact family friends in Hawaii, Lew and Dorothy Reiss. Through a complicated series of agreements between my mother in Austria, New York Catholic Social Services and Hawaii, I was able to join 'my American family' four months later. The Reiss' daughter, Lois, paid for my plane fare with the savings from her first year of teaching."

Contact with her mother was made possible by monthly messages limited to 25 words that were arranged by the Red Cross. "I will always be grateful to the Red Cross for those messages," she said.

But her ordeal was not over, for on December 7, 1941, she was in Honolulu. "Overnight, I was designated an 'enemy alien' since my German passport showed no proof of my Jewish ancestry," she said. "I was placed in a concentration camp in Honolulu, along with other German citizens and some Japanese citizens.

"The seven weeks of confinement gave me a lot of insight into the American way of life. I knew that some of my relatives had disappeared into Nazi concentration camps, but I was unwilling to believe the full breadth of the atrocities. What was fact, fiction or propaganda?

"But the way we were treated in the camp in Honolulu—the matron and the guards so hospitable, with shelter and food and a clean environment—made me realize that personal feelings were greatly respected by the American people even in times of war. And for the first time, I began to think that maybe this country would become my own and that maybe, eventually, I would want to be a citizen."

Not only did Dr. Barrows become an American citizen, but so did her father, mother and sister.

Ron Dunin, center, while in Budapest during his attempt to join Polish forces in France.
Photo courtesy of Ron Dunin.

Stan Harth

SLO MAYOR FOUGHT NAZIS, MANAGED GREAT ESCAPE

The flesh and blood of men and horses went up against the steel of tanks and armored vehicles during that first week of September of 1939, when Germany invaded Poland and plunged Europe into war.

Supporting the cavalry's charge as a second lieutenant in the Polish artillery was a man who became the Mayor of San Luis Obispo, Ron Dunin.

The German blitzkrieg, a combined attack of artillery, armored vehicles and air power, shattered the Polish army. Those who survived were urged to escape and to try to join Polish forces in France, which had yet to enter the war.

That is Dunin's story of courage, suffering and guile.

First, he escaped from a German prisoner of war camp and returned to Poland. There he was warned that his recapture was imminent. Because Germany is between Poland and France, he, his brother and three cousins developed a plan to escape by going south through Czechoslovakia, Hungary and Yugoslavia to gain access to the Adriatic Sea and from there the Mediterranean.

Dunin had a contact in Czechoslovakia, but they were betrayed there and arrested by a civilian police force associated with the Nazis. However, the commander of the patrol was not a Nazi and told Dunin and his associates how to escape. "We talked in Latin," Dunin said, "so that no one could understand that he was helping us."

But it wasn't easy. For it was winter, and the landscape was covered with ice and snow. They were chased by a patrol with dogs and had to travel through streams of almost frozen water to hide their tracks and scent. At one point, Dunin fell down a steep embankment and severely injured his back. "But I was in my twenties," he said, "and could keep going." However, some of that back trouble has stayed with him through the years.

Deep forests lined the river that formed the border between Czechoslovakia and Hungary. Traveling through them in the darkness of night was difficult. "We'd come out of the trees and think we had made it, then discover we hadn't and have to go back into the trees again and keep going," Dunin said.

All the time, they were listening for bells—sleigh bells—as they had been told that the border patrols traveled in sleighs.

Ron Dunin, right, after his successful escape from the Nazis. *Photo courtesy of Ron Dunin.*

Then they got lucky, making contact with the "underground," fighters for freedom who would help them. For purposes of concealment, their party of five was divided, with Dunin, his brother and one cousin going on to Budapest, while the two other cousins tried a different route. Both groups were guided and helped by the underground.

In Budapest, they traveled through subterranean tunnels that connected the buildings. "Once, we ended up next to the building where the Gestapo headquarters was," Dunin said. "It was a odd feeling."

Next came the attempt to get to Yugoslavia. "When we got to the River Drava on the border, we were in two groups," Dunin said. "I was in the second one. Half of the 21 men in the first party drowned trying to cross into Yugoslavia. Our guides took us to another place along the river and we got across okay."

But Dunin and his cousin were arrested by Yugoslavian border guards and locked up in a wooden jail. "It was strange," he recalled, "but we could hear the guards saying things like 'if they only knew that the board in the far back corner is loose' and 'if they only knew about the train that will pass by' at such-and-such a time. Our languages are similar, and I could understand them. And finally I realized what they meant."

That night, Dunin shoved against the designated board and soon they were on their way again. They made contact with the underground, received forged visas identifying them as French students and crossed the Adriatic Sea in the bottom of a rust bucket of a cargo ship to Italy. Then aboard the same ship they traveled through the Mediterranean Sea to the French port city of Marseilles.

There, Dunin was arrested again. This time because he lacked valid papers and couldn't prove his identity. He was shipped to a camp, then released, only to be arrested again in Paris. "I couldn't speak French and I had this dirty old hat I'd been wearing and one day I just threw it away," Dunin said. "Someone was suspicious about me and picked up the hat. It had some lettering in it, lettering like the size or where it was made, something like that. They thought I was passing a secret message and arrested me."

Finally, with the help of other Polish soldiers who had made it to France, Dunin was able to establish his identity and get back into uniform. The Poles were assigned to serve as support troops behind the Maginot Line. "We were behind the line and not even regimented (formed into units) then," he said.

When the Polish troops were sent to the port city of La Rochelle for evacuation to England, Dunin had still another close call. "We were in lines boarding two ships that were side by side," he said. "A Polish colonel with two large bags was somewhat ahead of me. When the ship's officers told him that he couldn't take such luggage aboard, the colonel began to argue and stopped the loading. So I boarded the other ship. Then the German Stukas (dive bombers) attacked and sank that other ship. I don't know how many were lost because we sailed away."

The ship landed at Plymouth. Dunin was assigned to Liverpool, then shipped to Glasgow, Scotland, where the troops slept in tents on what had been a dog racing track. Without knowing it, he had something of an affinity with San Luis Obispo even then, for the winter of 1940-41 was a particularly rainy one in both San Luis and Glasgow.

Dunin eventually was billeted as an adjutant of the Polish Artillery Academy.

WARTIME HUMOR (includes original spelling) _____

There isn't a soldier in this camp that don't posess some kind of knowledge, BUT, there is an uncountable amount of boys that do not posess this knowledge. How to lighten your burden on your hikes. For instance, you weigh 180 pounds, when you should weigh 150, you are carrying 30 pounds of lead on top of your equipment, savy, WHY suffer from excess lead when it can be easily and painlessly extracted, SO, TO THE FIELD HOUSE (gym). —*SHOT 'N SHELL*, May 13, 1942

Flavienne David Adams, fourth from the right, with her fellow students at Midwife Training Hospital de la Conception in Marseilles, France. *Photo courtesy of Flavienne Adams.*

Flavienne David Adams, left, on a street in Marseilles with her friend Jeanette. *Photo courtesy of Flavienne Adams.*

Liz Krieger

FUTURE FRENCH WAR BRIDE JOINS ANTI-NAZI UNDERGROUND

A beautiful but disconsolate young mother, a student friend caught up in a Nazi 'voluntary service' roundup and the deeply embedded teaching of some Catholic sisters in an orphanage would propel Flavienne David Adams into the fight against Hitler and his puppet government in Vichy France.

Flavienne began her long sojourn in the French underground as a midwife in a hospital in Marseilles.

"Before the war I had no idea who was Jewish or not. It wasn't something I was aware of."

Then Flavienne met up with "a very beautiful, very sad and uncommunicative" nineteen year old Jewish mother. "The birth of a healthy baby was usually a very exhilarating experience for mother and midwife alike. But this young woman was stony faced and refused to look at the baby. She didn't want to hold or nurse him. Finally, after a few days of my trying to tell her about her lovely baby boy, she told me her story."

"She had been an art student in Paris when she was picked up in a raid and put in a camp near Paris. One of the German guards fell in love with her and promised he would get her out. When she became pregnant and it became obvious, he did manage to get her out."

Her family had already fled from Paris to Bordeaux in Vichy France. "She didn't want her family to see her pregnant by a German soldier and was ashamed. And now, where was she to go? How could she possibly hide her baby? She just couldn't have any feeling for the child because for her he represented all the hatred, pain and humiliation she had gone through."

"But she was concerned about the child and wanted to somehow protect him. So she asked me if I would go see the hospital chaplain and ask that the baby be baptized. Then, she hoped, he wouldn't be identified as Jewish, someone might be willing to adopt him, and he wouldn't be subject to the same hunting that she was."

When Flavienne approached the priest, he refused. He reasoned that he couldn't baptize the child in good conscience, since it would be a lie because the baby's mother was Jewish. The child would have to decide for himself and he wasn't old enough. Meanwhile the baby would be left at the hospital for possible adoption.

"We didn't know about the German extermination camps then, but there was a feeling...I felt such great compassion, such pity for the girl and her child. This was my first direct experience of some innocent like this girl being put in a camp, subjected to sexual abuse, my first real awareness of the danger Jewish people faced."

"A few months later, I was confronted by another tragedy, that of my friend, Rene. His father had died when he was a boy. In the late 1930s Rene had been a student activist. He wasn't Jewish, but he might have been mistrusted by the authorities."

Early in 1942 Rene was caught in a raid in Marseilles.

When the war between France and Germany ended with the surrender of France in June, 1940, there were about a million French war prisoners in Germany, Flavienne recalls. Germany needed men to work in factories, farms and mines as it continued its war effort. So the call and promise went out: young Frenchmen to engage in 'voluntary service' in Germany. In return, the Nazis would release a like number of prisoners.

"At the first call for 'volunteers,' many really signed up. But after a few months it was obvious that the only prisoners the Germans were releasing were a few very sick or badly wounded. So, to meet its quota, the Vichy police started blocking off city streets, going from house to house, checking everybody's IDs. 'Volunteers' were 'selected' in the roundup, and my friend was taken."

"Rene called me, asking me to warn his mother to fix a suitcase and bring it to the place where they were kept. The 'volunteers' would have half an hour, 7-7:30 p.m., to say goodbye to their families."

"I didn't want to call his mother, she'd be so upset. So I went over and helped her fix a suitcase with a change of clothing and toilet articles—it could only be a small case—and bring her to say goodbye."

"I went and this was my first experience of seeing such a large group of people in such a desolate, grief-ridden atmosphere, like being caught up in a storm of grief. And the fear and helplessness. You didn't even believe such things happened. There were young women with babies, and crying, so many tears. Parents saying goodbye and nobody knowing what was going to happen next, when or if they'd see each other again. And many of them didn't. My friend didn't survive."

"The press was already very much controlled. It didn't report forced 'voluntary service' roundups. We heard rumors, but they were so fantastic you didn't believe them." As Flavienne left Rene, she was "absolutely stunned, in shock. I couldn't believe what I had seen and what it implied."

On her way home along a main street, "I met a group of teenagers, boys and girls, wearing the dark blue uniform of the new youth movement created by the Vichy government."

"They were singing joyfully, full of some kind of 'patriotic' song. I felt such a surge of hatred for those children, teenagers, that if I had a machine gun, I would have killed them."

"I became ashamed of myself, ashamed to discover so much violence in myself. They were just kids being indoctrinated in something which seemed to completely ignore the human suffering I had just experienced a few minutes ago."

As a result of the same raid in which Rene was taken, Flavienne and her mother hid a Jewish woman and her two children in the coal cellar beneath her mother's dry cleaning shop and apartment on the first floor of a five-story building.

Her husband had been captured in the raid, and now she was frantic. If she and the children returned to their apartment, in all likelihood they would be taken also.

"They stayed with us about two weeks. There was constant traffic through the shop and the staircase next to it. The police would come unannounced. Anyone was subject to a search. So during the day the Jewish family stayed in the cellar. As soon as the shop was closed, they would come up, have dinner with us and we would put mattresses on the floor for the children. She had my bed and I slept with my mother."

"Eventually the family was able to join relatives in a small village. What happened to them later we never knew."

Why, I asked Flavienne, did she help this family? Was she from a close, accepting family, a family of faith like the Huguenots of the French village of Le Chambon who successfully hid hundreds of Jews?

On the contrary, she said. She had been raised in a Catholic orphanage from the age of four until she was fourteen, thanks to her parents' separation at the end of World War I. "The nuns were very restrictive, chauvinistic and intolerant of anything not strictly Catholic. Many of the sisters came from poor families and were themselves mainly orphans with little education. They knew little of the cultural environment outside of their religion."

"In spite of the lack of tenderness and understanding of some of the sisters, I realize that they instilled in me a belief in my immortal soul and the fact that I was responsible for it."

"All through my life when decisions were difficult to make, this feeling of this precious part of me, a soul, that I should not tarnish it, helped me to make the right choice. Every day I have felt blessed in this gift from the sisters, for it has given me the courage to do what I may not have done otherwise."

But Flavienne emphasizes that she did not make a conscious decision to help the cellar family and the countless others she would later assist

Flavienne David Adams and her husband, Phil. *Photo courtesy of Flavienne Adams.*

"outside of the law."

"You don't decide to get involved. You just become involved because people around you need help."

Such was the disillusionment of the war years that Flavienne wasn't certain God existed. "But I had to care about others because I still knew I had a soul!"

Today Flavienne lives in San Luis Obispo with her husband, Phil Adams, Professor of Economics at Cal Poly. They met in France at the end of the war.

Susi Steiner

MANY MOVIES HELPED HER TO LEARN ENGLISH

I wanted to be a doctor, but Hitler intervened.

Born in Vienna in 1915, I had attended grammar and high schools there and had attended the University of Vienna Medical School for four and one-half years.

Then came Hitler's invasion of Austria on March 12, 1938. The next day, all schools had big signs posted that declared, "Jews no longer admitted." My younger sister and I left immediately.

We were able to say good bye to our parents and to a brother and a sister but not to other relatives and friends. And as we left, we wondered if we would ever see them again.

After we arrived in Italy, we immediately applied for a visa to the United States, and on June 16, 1938, we arrived in New York City. My sister left the next day for San Francisco.

While I spoke German, Italian and French and knew Latin, I did not speak English. And I had only $12 in my pocket. But I was able to secure a job as a governess for room and board and $60 per month. And I rapidly learned English, in part by spending most of my days off in movie theaters and watching the same film three or four times.

After two years in this country, I joined with a friend in catering parties for children. Then I learned to be a puppeteer and entertainer for those parties.

In the meantime, my parents and youngest sister had settled in San Francisco. So I joined them and got a job in a sandwich factory. I also helped my mother with her catering business. This was a sideline for her, as she was a musician and piano teacher. And I continued to perform as a puppeteer.

I was never able to complete my medical education.

The Editors

EXPERIENCES WITH PREWAR JAPAN TOLD BY LOCALS

When a father admits he erred, a son listens. And Kiyoshi Sakurai certainly did.

He was nine years old when his parents took their family to Japan in February of 1941 after the family business failed.

Almost immediately, he said, his father realized he had made a "giant mistake." He added, "Father was drafted into the Japanese army, and he would tell us, 'I wish I could break a leg so I wouldn't be accepted'."

Added to the frightening atmosphere of Japan's military adventures, according to Kiyoshi, was the way the family from America was treated. "The local people's attitude toward my family was 'Yankee, Go Home.'"

But they couldn't. For, as the *Telegram-Tribune* reported on August 16, 1941, the United States State Department disclosed that Japan was refusing permission for American ships like the *President Coolidge* to call at Japanese ports to pick up Americans who desired to return to this country.

Fred Artindale of San Luis Obispo soon couldn't leave Asia either. In December of 1941, he had just completed his second concert as a violinist in the Shanghai Municipal Orchestra in that international city when war broke out between Great Britain and Japan. The Japanese occupied Shanghai.

A third generation resident who was born in that city in 1904, he had become Secretary of Geddes & Co., Ltd., an import/export firm, and was a creator of beautiful violins and cellos as well as a repairer and restorer of stringed instruments.

"Like me, my wife, Bertha, was born to a Eurasian mother," he said. "The fact that her father was German almost led to her deportation prior to the Japanese takeover of Shanghai. Her father and brother had to go to Germany. Since she was married to a British citizen, she got to stay.

"During the Japanese occupation, I was forced to wear a red arm band with a black 'B,' for 'British' on it. Americans had an 'A' on their red arm bands. We really had no trouble with the Japanese. Each private company had a Japanese supervisor. We didn't talk to him much. He came and sat and looked at our work and went off. The food situation was adequate."

Paul Kurokawa, a native of San Luis Obispo, knew the stresses of a Japan at war early on, for after graduation from San Luis High School, he

Paul Kurokawa, a SLO native, and a friend show Tokyo to Howard and Fred Louis, members of the Ah Louis family. *Photo courtesy of Paul Kurokawa.*

Betty and Paul Kurokawa met on a boat returning from Japan in February, 1941. They were married six months later. *Photo courtesy of Paul Kurokawa.*

had gone to Japan to study political economy in the business division of Meiji University in Tokyo. He had done so as a matter of economics: he couldn't afford to attend the University of California as he had hoped, but he could stretch $25 a month to attend Meiji.

Shortly after his arrival in Tokyo in the autumn of 1934, he heard that some prominent visitors from San Luis Obispo were stopping by the seaport city of Yokohama after their trip to China. He went there and visited with Fred (now Col. USA, Ret.) and Howard "Toby" Louis, sons of Ah Louis, the San Luis labor contractor, farmer and merchant.

Since Japan's invasion of Manchuria had badly damaged its relations with China, Paul exchanged his Meiji University uniform with Toby when they got off the ship. This was a considerable risk for Paul as he could have spent a long time in prison for smuggling two persons of Chinese ancestry off the ship to sightsee in Yokohama and Tokyo. But Paul was thinking like the American he is.

After his graduation, he was involved with international trade, including having an American football team visit Japan, until the winter of 1940-41, when the American ambassador, Joseph Grove, warned all American citizens to leave Japan. He met his wife, Betty, while aboard the ship going home. She, too, was an American who had been studying in Japan.

WARTIME HUMOR

"Diogenese" asks:
"Now that we have electricity in Baywood, what shall I do with my lantern?
Answer: Save it for the German people—they'll soon be searching for an honest leader.
—*Baywood Park Observer*
Spring Issue, 1942

To Women Facing Rationing:
"It won't be so bad, after all. If you eat less sugar then you won't need the rubber girdles you won't be able to get. Hips, hips, hooray!
—"Sam Luis" column
Telegram-Tribune
February 24, 1942

Part 3

KINDNESS ON THE CENTRAL COAST

"Four-Star General" Ran Phone Exchange

San Luis Obispo entered the war with a highly antiquated telephone system. Photo courtesy Grace Mulkey.

When I look back, I remember the telephone office was so unprepared to give service to the thousands of men coming into Camp San Luis. I wonder how we lived through it, but we did.

After Pearl Harbor, when we went to work we never were sure what time we would get off work. Our chief operator would work from 8 a.m. to 5 p.m. and then would come back at 7 p.m. and would not go home until 10 or 11 p.m.

She was truly a four-star general, one who never received a star. And her husband should have received a medal for staying home night after night alone. There was no television then to help pass the time.

I was going home about 10 o'clock one night and was parked in back of the Christian Church next to the post office. When I drove around the church, I slammed on my brakes. The San Luis Obispo Post Office was surrounded by soldiers who were standing on guard with rifles and bayonets. Their white helmets shone brightly in my headlights. There were two large Army trucks parked at the back of the post office.

Well, I really got away from there fast. The next day I was told that the payroll for 40,000 men had come through the post office and had to be transferred to Camp San Luis.

Every night was hectic until we had more equipment installed and more operators to handle the calls. There were a lot of soldiers from the East and South, and we had several of their wives working who had transferred here to be with their husbands. Some of the names of the towns we had calls to were as hard to pronounce as our Spanish names were for them. We discovered that those operators were having no trouble getting their calls through to the East Coast; so they were put on the boards handling those calls. It was really funny because they could understand their dialect and could pronounce the names of the towns.

So until the war was over and things slowly returned to normal, I would say the telephone operators who handled the calls from all the camps everywhere were very much involved in the war effort.

—Grace Mulkey, Operator #17
La Vista, Vol. 4, No. 2

Evangeline "Jean" Kirk

"SIT DOWN OVER THERE," HE WOULD SAY STERNLY

My parents, Joaquin and Francisca Craveiro, moved to San Luis Obispo in November of 1938 to buy the Golden West Restaurant from Mary Serpa. Two weeks later, my husband and I and our two sons, two and four years old, joined them as partners in the business.

The Golden West Restaurant was at 676 Higuera Street, where there is now an empty lot.

My father didn't smile much except when he talked about the times he went whaling with older men from the island of Pico Azores when he was 18 to 20 years old. He came to America when he was 20 or 21. After working hard in the San Joaquin Valley to learn how to farm and milk cows, he asked his fiancée, my mother, to join him. They were married in Hanford in 1912. I was born the following year, and my brother, Joaquin Jr., was born in 1917.

Restaurant work was hard. We had a family-type place and menu. When a depression era "hobo" or "tramp"—as they were called—came into the restaurant to ask for something to eat, my father would say, "Sit down over there," indicating a stool at the counter. He then would give the person a bowl of soup, two slices of French bread and coffee. This happened many times.

When dad was busy in the back room, I did the cooking and served the booths and persons at the counter as well. We cooked in back of the counter and near the front door so customers and potential customers could see what was being cooked.

Joaquin Jr. went into the military service on November 11, 1941. Our restaurant was very busy because of the development of Camp San Luis Obispo. Mother could be there only part-time because she took care of my sons, Larry and Ronnie Souza, but she baked pies and puddings for the restaurant.

While our main waitress was my cousin, Aldora Craveiro Santos, all of the other waitresses were the wives of soldiers. Our place was a sea of soldiers. It was hard to tell when a soldier had finished eating and left because another one would immediately take his place before the table or counter could be cleaned.

I recall a time when a soldier and his wife were talking with my dad

"The Man with the Stern Look" almost smiled in this photo. With Joaquin Sr. are, from left, his wife, Francisca, a waitress named Jackie and Jean Kirk. *Photo courtesy of Jean Kirk.*

about being on a two-week furlough but without the funds to go to their hometown for a visit. Dad and I felt sorry for them but we ourselves were just making ends meet. After the couple ate, they left. Dad turned to me and said, "I ought to help those poor kids. Go after them." I did, and dad loaned them $100. We never heard from them again.

The soldiers' wives who were waitresses had three meals a day as part of their jobs, but many of the wives who weren't working would sleep in until late in the morning so they would only eat two meals a day. Many went for walks and picked vegetables and fruit from the gardens of residents.

Dad always looked serious, and a lot of our customers would come in and greet him by saying, "Hello, Boss, what are you mad about today?"

Waitresses were lucky to get a 25-cent tip from each table, and sometimes we would get a one dollar tip for serving a table of six or eight persons.

WARTIME HUMOR

Remember our "Skip the Blond, Buy a Bond" slogan?

Well, the Associated Press picked it up and gave it a nice ride in the newspapers, and repercussions are being heard from far and near.

Our choice comes from North Little Rock, Arkansas, a post-card with our item pasted neatly on the back, with the following message scrawled across the bottom in a bold feminine hand:

"Skip the blond, buy a bond! Why not armloads of both?"

Well, why not?   —*SHOT 'N SHELL*, April 15, 1942

Aldora Craveiro Santos

FOR SOME SOLDIERS' WIVES: WARM MEALS AND MONEY

I went to work at the Golden West Restaurant when my cousin, Joaquin Craveiro Jr., was inducted into the military in November of 1941, and I worked there for the duration of the war.

My father, Leonard Craveiro, was Uncle Joaquin's brother, and my mother, Josefa, was Aunt Francesca's sister. My uncle and aunt were co-owners of the restaurant with their children, Evangeline (Jean) and Joaquin Jr.

Those were hard years for everyone. All the young men were gone, including my husband, John, who was then my fiancé. But we did our best to keep things going.

I would transport the milk from my father's dairy to the creamery and then go to work at the restaurant.

Uncle Joaquin was a good, compassionate man who always was ready to help those in need. And when he fed a needy person for free at the restaurant he would have that person sit at the counter rather than in the back room or outside.

And he helped many soldiers' wives, many of whom were left behind when their husbands shipped out for overseas. They would come in for a cup of coffee, and we would talk. When he heard their stories, he would give them a warm meal and often he would give them money.

I particularly remember the time a girl came in who was pregnant, alone, without a job and far from home. When he heard her story, uncle gave her train fare to get home.

I don't think he was ever repaid for his generosity; he didn't expect it, and he never talked about it.

In thanksgiving for the end of the war and for the safe return of Joaquin Jr., Uncle Joaquin and Aunt Francesca donated the Statue of Our Lady of Fatima that is in the alcove of Old Mission Church.

WARTIME HUMOR

"Did you get a rating?"
"Last month or this month?"
"Either one."
"No."

—*SHOT 'N SHELL*, May 20, 1942

THAT WINTER
WAS TRULY A DIRTY ONE

It really rained in 1941 when construction was underway at Camp San Luis. That's why the town was so dirty. It never had been that way before, and it certainly hasn't been that way since. Every restaurant, store and barber shop had mud tracked in from the streets.

—Elsie Muzio
La Vista, Vol. 4, No. 2

THERE WAS A TIME
WHEN ANY ROOM WOULD DO

After Pearl Harbor, the men who were sent to Camp San Luis were aware that this was their last training period before going overseas.

The loved ones of the soldiers converged on San Luis Obispo to spend precious moments with them. But there were not enough hotel rooms to accommodate them, so local residents with extra rooms rented them to these civilians. There was such a need that it was said they would rent a "chicken coop." In most cases, residents were patriotic and didn't charge excessive rates.

Our first rental was a 16-foot plywood trailer in our backyard. Then a "little bedroom" off our back porch was made available. Finally, we moved our twins in their bassinets and Charles in his crib into our large bedroom, and had a second bedroom for rent.

We all used one bathroom, and the people from the back had to come through our kitchen to get to it.

You could count on a houseful of people and children when you came to visit us during those years.

—Eleanor Brown
La Vista, Vol. 4, No. 2

Alice E. Dulitz

ATASCADERAN RECALLS AIDING ARMY COUPLE

During the construction of Camp Roberts I was working for the Santa Maria Gas Company in Paso Robles and living in Atascadero. I made the commute with workers from the camp who lived in the area. There was so much rain that it seemed my car's windshield wipers never got a rest, and there was so much mud on the roads that my windshield often looked like frosted glass.

When the camp was ready, the first soldiers who came were from the Utah National Guard. Residents of the North County area had been urged to help provide housing for the soldiers' families. My father and I lived in a comfortable three-bedroom house, so I obtained a loan and built an additional bathroom and outside entrance for tenants.

Our first tenants were an officer and his wife from Ogden, Utah. When some of my friends expressed concern that the tenants might be Mormon, I said that I hoped they were. For, having lived for a number of years in an old Mormon community in southern Idaho, I knew what fine people Mormons are, and I knew they would not drink, smoke or carouse.

And that couple was just as I expected. While the original rental agreement was just for a room in which to sleep and a bathroom, I couldn't accept the fact that the officer's wife would have to go to town to eat her meals alone. So we worked out an arrangement for her to use the kitchen. This then evolved into a very friendly contest over shopping and food preparation and over who could do more than her share. And it became a joke among us that her husband usually managed to get home by dessert time.

When the first of the couple's two sons was about to be born, we agreed that one room wasn't sufficient in which to raise a baby. Since I worked for the gas company, I would learn early on when anyone was moving. So I was able to locate an apartment for the couple in Paso Robles. Later I practically ran a rental agency this way!

And when that first couple moved away from our home, "grandpa"—as the couple had come to call my father—and I sat on the edge of a bed and cried.

Stan Harth

COUNTY GEARED UP EARLY TO ENTERTAIN SERVICEMEN

Even before Pearl Harbor, San Luis Obispo was trying to provide entertainment facilities for the increasing number of servicemen in the area.

And, as the war years came, some young ladies in San Luis Obispo were trying to comply with a certain rule of the local USO (United Service Organization).

Here's how Margaret Coyner describes it: "There was this silly rule at the USO on Santa Rosa and Mill Streets that the girls couldn't dance unless they wore silk stockings—and these were impossible to come by! So, some of the girls would cheat by wearing liquid leg make-up. And then for the seam in the back of the stocking, the girls would take an eyebrow pencil and run a line up the back of one another's legs." She adds, "The nicest girls in town were recruited to work at the USOs. Their parents were really fussy about them, and they were chaperoned to death. No liquor was allowed inside the USOs, and the girls were not allowed to leave with the soldiers."

How San Luis Obispo geared up to provide entertainment facilities can be traced from stories appearing in the *Telegram-Tribune* in 1941.

A March 21 story reported that more than 25 clubs and organizations in San Luis Obispo were involved in providing recreation for soldiers. The Rotary, Lions and Kiwanis Clubs were among these, and the S.L.O. Exchange Club had a "take-a-soldier-home-to-dinner" project.

The Business and Professional Women's Club, according to a story on March 24, would be responsible for finding girls to attend dances at the "Soldier's Hut." This recreation hall at 1043 Nipomo St. was made possible through the cooperation of the county, the city and the local American Legion Post, said a March 28 story.

The libraries were swinging into action too. On March 24, it was announced that the county library in the courthouse would be kept open from 7 to 9 p.m. on Wednesdays as a service to soldiers. By May 9, this was changed to Saturday evenings to benefit more soldiers. And Abbie Kellogg, the City Librarian, announced that the library at Monterey and Broad Streets would be open from 2 to 5 p.m. on Sundays.

A property tax measure to provide additional funds for the City Parks and Recreation Department was approved by a 5 to 1 margin in April. And by June 4, a new USO center for white soldiers was proposed for Mill and

This USO in San Luis Obispo was on Higuera across from Court Street. *Photo courtesy of San Luis Obispo County Historical Museum.*

Dick Willett, YMCA director, and Myarl Clark, a local teacher, lead singing. *Photo courtesy of San Luis Obispo County Historical Museum.*

Santa Rosa Streets, and a local fund drive for it was initiated. The former USO facility at Morro and Palm Streets would eventually serve Afro-Americans.

The need for a USO was featured on July 7 with a photo of a soldier leaning against a lamppost and these words: "With thousands of soldiers training near small towns, many a trooper like this one can't even find a place to sit when he gets leave from camp. It may only be a step from this lamppost to a saloon or gambling place. The United Services Organization is going to remedy that. Soon there will be a spacious, home-like USO service club offering this soldier wholesome recreation and guidance. The S.L.O. campaign for funds will go forward Thursday and Friday of this week."

Among those in the leadership of the campaign were Supervisor Richard L. Willett, Mayor Fred Kimball, Bill O'Donnell, Mrs. Emma Kelker, J.J. Van Harreveld and O. F. Lucksinger, as reported on July 9.

Meanwhile, local religious groups were taking turns serving coffee and punch to servicemen at what was called "the local Army-Navy YMCA." In a story on July 21, the *T-T* reported the Central Coast Section of the National Council of Jewish Women had served some 400 soldiers there and that a Presbyterian group was to provide the service the next week.

As for the USO campaign, Supervisor Willett had set a quota of $1,600 for citizen participation. That goal was far exceeded by the $4,200 reported contributed by August 27.

And on December 22, the *T-T* carried a story that reported the dedication on the previous day of USO centers in San Luis Obispo, Paso Robles and San Miguel.

Included in the USO center at Santa Rosa and Mill Streets were the YMCA, National Catholic Community Service, Jewish Welfare Board and the Travelers Aid.

It was during this period that Mitchell Park was proposed. On November 20, Mayor Kimball spoke of plans to buy the unused school lot bounded by Buchon, Santa Rosa, Osos and Pismo Streets and to landscape it for a public park.

The following appeared in the *T-T* on December 20: "A pre-Christmas party was given to bring cheer to the patients in the station hospital, Camp San Luis Obispo, by townspeople in cooperation with the Red Cross. It was held in the Red Cross recreational building at the hospital. Major arrangements were handled by Mrs. G. D. Kelker and Miss Ethel Cooley...The auditorium was beautifully decorated...During the afternoon, the Tri-Y girls, chaperoned by Miss Cooley, joined the convalescent patients for games and dancing and also provided refreshments of hot chocolate and

Young women of Motor Corps in 1941. Bottom row, left to right: Betty Shakell, Florence Grundell, Patty Kaiser Eister. Second row: Pearl Mallagh, Margaret Maxwell, Grace Dickey Brown, Ruth Preuss. Third row: Polly Sauer, Bea Kaiser, Margaret Cooper, Ethel Cooley. Fourth row: Winnie Gist Root, Margaret Ditmas Coyner, Mable Dunklee. *Photo courtesy of Margaret Coyner.*

homemade cookies...The Red Cross Motor Corps provided the transportation for the Tri-Y members."

The new City Librarian, Doris Garcelon, announced on January 12, 1942, a "Victory Book" campaign to provide books to fill USO centers as part of a nationwide drive by the American Library Association.

Dorothy Hoover Thomson of San Luis noted that her USO days included shopping and writing letters for soldiers in the hospital and inviting many of them to her home for food and music.

And this, perhaps, was the most typical way of all that the residents of San Luis Obispo reached out to show how much they cared about the sons of others.

This story first appeared in La Vista, Vol. 4, No. 2.

Larry Souza

SHOESHINE BOY LEARNS TO DISCOUNT AD CLAIMS

Larry Souza, a shoeshine boy from age seven through 11, in his First Communion outfit. *Photo courtesy of Larry Souza.*

My parents and grandparents operated the Golden West Restaurant in the 600 block of Higuera Street in San Luis Obispo, but while still a boy I went into business for myself.

For Camp San Luis Obispo was full of soldiers and so were the downtown streets. Like many other boys, I built a shoe-shine box and sold shines on the streets for a dime. One day I sold 30 shines.

Then came the day when I discovered a new type of liquid shoe polish that was described as "self-shining." To me that meant less work for the same price. My first customer after I bought a bottle of the new polish was an army officer. I dusted his shoes, applied the liquid and asked for a dime.

"Aren't you going to buff my shoes?" he asked.

I held up the bottle and pointed to the label and said, "See? Self-shining."

With a doubtful grin, he said, "Okay," and paid me and went on his way.

A few minutes later he returned and showed me his shoes upon which the liquid had dried, producing a dull, brown surface. "Buff these!" he ordered. And I did.

Before the war years there had been times when my dad and brother and I would sit on the curb and watch the occasional vehicle go by on Higuera Street. Occasionally we would see refugees from the Dust Bowl drive by with their belongings tied to the top and on the back of their dilapidated cars. But the war years changed all that.

Famed Pianist Hosted Dances

Ignace Jan Paderewski in an 1897 photo. Paderewski owned a ranch west of Paso Robles and spent much time at the elegant hotel in town. *Photo courtesy of the San Luis Obispo County Historical Museum.*

The war in Europe seemed particularly close for Elsa and Donald Orcutt as they swirled around the dance floor of the elegant Paso Robles Hotel.

After Hitler's invasion of his beloved Poland in September of 1939, Ignace Jan Paderewski, a guest at the hotel who was a famed pianist and a premier of Poland during World War I, sought to raise funds for Polish war relief. As owners of a ranch in the county, he and his wife hosted several dances at the hotel.

Then came a night which ended those events. Here's how Elsa Hewitt recalls it:

"For the first time in years, the hotel was full, mostly with army personnel and construction people pouring over plans for the proposed nearby Camp Roberts.

"Suddenly one night, clear and cold, the fire sirens boomed. The hotel was ablaze. It presumably was started by someone putting linens down a laundry shoot and accidentally dropping a lighted cigarette.

"My husband was one of the volunteer firemen who worked all night on that blaze. Their rubber coats were melting in front from the heat and stiff in the back from the cold.... Had there been any breeze at all, the entire town would have been in cinders the next morning."

—*Elsa Orcutt Hewitt*

Dora Lammer Harter

HANCOCK PHONE OPERATOR SAW PILOTS' JOYS, SORROWS

Strange things tended to happen to telephone calls to Allan Hancock College of Aeronautics in October of 1941, for that is when I went to work there operating the manual switchboard.

It was a very busy switchboard, with many incoming calls, including ones from Washington, D.C. At first, I often pulled the wrong cords and disconnected calls. When this happened, someone would come out into the main office in a huff, and I would have to scramble to try to re-establish the broken connection. Eventually, I became more efficient and such problems became a thing of the past.

The switchboard remained open until the control tower notified me that all the planes had landed. One day when I had not heard from the tower well past 5:30 p.m., I contacted it and was told that a plane was missing and that I would be contacted when it arrived. About half an hour later, the tower telephoned me and asked me to start calling people to drive their cars to the airport and to form a ring around the landing strip so that the cars' headlights would provide light to help the pilot land. The response

Dora Lammer Harter operated a typewriter as well as a busy switchboard. *Photo courtesy of Dora Harter.*

was outstanding. Later it was reported that the pilot had landed without mishap at an auxiliary field.

We had a small PX (Post Exchange) in the office, and every time one of the cadets soloed, a crowd would accompany him to this store so that he could purchase a white scarf, an emblem of his solo flight. Contrasted with this were the occasions when a cadet "washed out"—was dismissed from flight training— and had to wait alone at an outside corner of the office building for his orders elsewhere.

My husband-to-be was an aircraft mechanic in the Air Corps Reserve at Hancock, and on December 7, 1941, we drove to Camp Roberts to visit my oldest brother, Tommy, who was an instructor there. (All four of my brothers served in the U.S. Armed Forces during World War II.) We did not learn of the attack on Pearl Harbor until we arrived at the camp, and we were not allowed to see Tommy. On our way back to Santa Maria, we picked up as many hitchhiking servicemen as we could to help them get back to their units.

My parents at that time lived on the Dos Pueblos Ranch north of Goleta. It was near Naples, a watering spot for the steam locomotives of the Southern Pacific Railroad, which has a very tall trestle bridge on the ranch. My two younger sisters, Anna and Barbara, helped the war effort by being members of a group which guarded that bridge because it was used so extensively by trains carrying troops.

WARTIME HUMOR

Grab The Rainbow!

A story circulating in the news informs us in the Service that our young ladies back home are falling for a fad of wearing a black ring to indicate a boyfriend in the Armed Service.

Please girls, please! Make it gay!

Take our old grand-dad, for instance.

Remember there was a day when he put that fine beaver hat, cowhide boots and frock coat on the shelf, and heeded his country's call!

He packed up his old musket and his mess kit, strapped on his powder horn, and away he went—off to the wars!

Did the gals he left behind wear a mourning black? They did not.

Instead, 'round their neck they wore a yellow ribbon—wore it for their lover who was far, far away.

For us, girls—make it a brilliant and flaming crimson! Turn to the rainbow—grab off a strand, something that will blend with your hair and your eyes!

Make it a blaze of glory!

That's for us!   —SHOT 'N SHELL, April 15, 1942

LUCKY JENNY'S STORY OF ENDURING FRIENDSHIPS ──────

Jenny Hiltel was lucky.

A doctor who worked at Camp San Luis Obispo lived next door to her during that winter of 1940-41.

When Jenny developed blood poisoning, she was rushed to San Luis General Hospital.

What she needed, Jenny recalls, was the new, powerful antibiotic, penicillin. But it was not available to civilians.

Somehow her doctor/neighbor was able to obtain the precious medicine and to have it delivered to the hospital. What's more, Jenny recalls, "The doctor even got a young army wife to take care of me and my two children after I came home from the hospital."

Jenny is now 82 years old. And that army wife and she still correspond. "We heard from her this year," says Jenny in some awe. "She still remembers that I made a special lunch for her."

She adds, "The war seemed to bring people together. The doctor in his Christmas letters still writes of how much our friendship meant to him and his wife when they were far from home.

"After the war, people went back to their own towns, but they still want to hang on to the kindness and friendship of the people of San Luis Obispo."

—Liz Krieger

WARTIME INTEREST ──────

Colored Troops' USO Club Opens...

J. Barksdale Brown, who is here from New York City to take charge of the USO for colored troops at 861 Palm Street, announces that the formal opening of the USO will be held Sunday, July 19.

Brown, who has an A.B. degree from Atlanta University and an M.A. from Columbia, is highly qualified for his new position as USO director....

He plans a wide program of activity for colored troops stationed at Camp San Luis Obispo, including dances, movies, games, etc. The USO will be equipped with ping pong tables, stationery, and "letters on a record" machines, he stated.

There will be a staff of professional and volunteer recreation directors.

—SHOT 'N SHELL
July, 1942

Bill Cattaneo

ARMISTICE DAY BECAME INDUCTION DAY FOR 42

Six young men in their late teens and early 20s were cruising about in an old jalopy, with the radio on, in September of 1939 in downtown San Luis Obispo.

From all outward appearances, this was merely another car loaded with young blades who were enjoying a casual weekend of driving, big band music and girl-watching.

But this was no ordinary summer weekend; it was the weekend of September 2, and the boys were not listening to Glenn Miller or Tommy Dorsey. They were awaiting word of the German reply to the ultimatum delivered by Britain's Prime Minister, Neville Chamberlain, after the German invasion of Poland on September 1.

The San Luis Obispo youths were all of military draft age, and they were painfully aware that if war was declared on Germany by England and France, they would most likely be in military uniforms before long.

One of these six young men was Anthony Louis Domingos, and with Tony, we begin our story of a special military induction event that took place in San Luis Obispo on November 11, 1941.

Tony was born in the San Luisito Creek region between San Luis and Morro Bay. His father, Antonio S. Domingos, who was born in the Azores, was a farmer and businessman. For years, he operated a livery stable at Marsh and Broad Streets. Tony's mother, Mary S. Machado, was born on the Price Ranch.

Tony attended Old Mission Grammar School and Mission High School from the second grade through his sophomore year. In 1935, when the high school was made into a girls-only institution, he transferred to San Luis Obispo High School for his junior year.

Tony's sisters, Mabel and Eleanor, and his brother, Edward, were graduated from San Luis High and moved to the San Francisco Bay Area for further schooling. Mrs. Domingos, a widow, also moved there with Tony, who was graduated from Berkeley High School in 1937.

After a year and one-half at the University of California at Berkeley, Tony returned to San Luis, where he worked until enrolling in San Luis Obispo Junior College in September of 1940. Starting in February of 1941, he worked the 3 a.m. shift at the Southern Pacific Railroad freight house while continuing to attend the junior college.

Then there was Joaquin Craveiro, Jr., whose family moved to San Luis in the fall of 1938 after selling a dairy in Visalia. One month after their arrival, Joaquin, his father and Tony Souza, a partner in the dairy, purchased the Golden West Restaurant on Higuera Street.

Joe Hudtloff came to San Luis in 1941 from the Ukiah area to attend a government school on advanced radio operation and repair that was conducted at Cal Poly.

Raymond Francis Horn, a 1934 graduate of San Luis High School, gained experience in a number of jobs before joining the Pacific Gas & Electric Co. in 1937.

Meanwhile in Europe, Hitler continued his barrage of threats and intimidation against Germany's neighbors. Winston Churchill led a small, unheeded chorus in the British Parliament about the need for military preparedness.

In Asia, Japan had conquered Manchuria in 1931 and now was about to take over the rest of China.

America, though outwardly neutral, was slowly awakening to the menace of global war.

On January 28, 1938, U.S. President Franklin D. Roosevelt asked Congress to expand the military, and on May 17th, the Naval Expansion Act was enacted. Then on September 16, 1940, the Selective Service Act was passed, providing for the draft of 900,000 men each year. It called for the compulsory registration of all males between 20 and 36 years of age. Originally, the length of service was to be one year, but in August of 1941, this was extended to a period of not more than 30 months in peacetime.

By November 11, 1941, 17 groups of San Luis youths had left for military induction. In those days, November 11th was observed annually as Armistice Day, marking the end of hostilities during World War I.

And it was on that day that San Luis honored 42 men who formed the largest contingent of military inductees to leave the city up to that time. They were from both San Luis and other parts of the county.

While Tony Domingos and Joaquin Craveiro, Jr., can't recall their reactions when their draft call-up notices arrived, Ray Horn certainly does. He said it was simply, "They're after me!" His induction was delayed for two weeks because of a severe sunburn he received at Avila.

Joe Hudtloff did not receive an induction notice; he was a volunteer.

These men and 38 others were honored at a special luncheon hosted by the San Luis Obispo County Board of Supervisors in the Veteran's Hall at the county courthouse. Al Ferrini presided, and Lt. Col. Lewis H. Jones, Judge Advocate General of California's 40th Division, gave the farewell address. More than 200 persons attended.

Newlyweds Joaquin and Eleanor Craveiro. *Photo courtesy of the Craveiros.*

None of the others can recall specifics about the event, but Horn remembers, "I didn't feel like eating."

After the luncheon, 40 men boarded a Greyhound bus for the trip to the Presidio of San Francisco.

Here is a list of those in the group: Joe Hudtloff, Robin Lindesmith, John Golden, James Brown, James Emmons, Cecil Brooks Berning, Marion Buss, Robert Knox, Leslie Machado, John Hathaway, Joe Isola, George Hosada, Anthony Louis Domingos, Tom Creager, Andrew McGovern, Arthur Reeves, Douglas M. Parsons, Ray Plunkett, Maurice Vanderberg, Charles Thompson, Rodney Meyers, Raymond Horn, Anthony Juarez, Tony Roza, Lewis Santos, Joaquin Craviero, Harold Ogg, Eugene Reis and Vernal Holden, all of San Luis, and, from other parts of the county, Felix Janolis, Delmar Holloway, Orville Schultz, Basil Bolling, Thomas Bewley, Seiren Ikeda, Raymond Dieball, Howard Cowen, Raymond Oscoria, Garth Gingrich and Lewis Flora.

After their preliminary induction, the men were sent by Southern Pacific passenger train to the Presidio of Monterey for further processing. Then the entire group was transferred to Camp Wallace at Galveston, Texas, for basic training before being sent as a group to Fort Bliss at El Paso.

From there they went their separate ways. Tony Domingos was in the medical service at Letterman Hospital in San Francisco. Joe Hudtloff's areas of duty ranged from the Aleutians to the Philippines and Okinawa. Craveiro was discharged from Fort Leavenworth, Kansas, and Raymond Horn went ashore on Utah Beach 21 days after D-Day on June 6, 1944.

Looking back, these men agree that when they entered the military service they expected it would be for only a short time. But what happened on the island of Oahu on December 7, 1941, changed all that.

Dan Krieger

HOW THE CENTRAL COAST WAITED, THEN REACTED

Fifty years ago, war had been raging in Europe for two years.

Tens of thousands of soldiers were being trained on the Central Coast at Camp Cooke (now Vandenberg Air Force Base), Camp San Luis Obispo and Camp Roberts.

The sleepy town of Morro Bay had just entered the world of preparedness for modern war with the dedication of a 12th Naval District section base during the last week of November of 1941.

It hadn't been a very good year for sports. The European War had canceled not only the 1940 Olympics but the 1941 Davis Cup and Wimbledon tennis matches as well. Lou Gehrig had died in June. Many colleges were considering dropping football, mainly because of the impact of Selective Service. But Joe DiMaggio had hit safely in 56 consecutive games, and there had been a World Series.

Life went on, but at a special pace. On American campuses, the young women sensed that the men would be leaving for the training camps of war and that they would be full-grown women before the troopships came home.

"God Bless America" by Kate Smith was Number 3 on the Lucky Strike Hit Parade, closely followed by the chanteuse Hildegarde's recording of "The White Cliffs of Dover."

War tensions surrounded the sun-baked hills of late autumn along the Central Coast. On Saturday, Dec. 6, 1941, the *San Luis Obispo Telegram-Tribune* featured an ominous sign of the times: A photograph of a London family ensconced in a sandbag dugout shelter with "Home Sweet Home" written over the entrance. The photo accompanied a column boldly titled "Staying Alive— Some Pointers for Americans on What to Do When and If Bombs Fall From the Skies."

On that same day, the *Telegram-Tribune* ran a photo and lengthy article on Clara King, daughter of Cal Poly's Frank J. King, who married Sgt. Robert Harvey Baldridge of San Luis in a simple ceremony at the Baptist Parsonage.

Residents of San Luis Obispo County's North Coast region braced for the winter storms. They sensed that Christmas 1941 was going to be different. Unprecedented tempests seemed likely as the fearsome war clouds loomed over the Pacific.

A number of ranchers and townspeople of Morro Bay, Cayucos and Cambria hoped that war could be avoided. Some even remained staunch isolationists, urging their fellow Americans to stay out of Europe's cauldron of troubles.

Patrick O'Brien of Cambria addressed these "America Firsters" in a letter to *The Cambrian* on November 27, 1941. Profoundly disturbed because so many of his fellow Irish-Americans had adopted a "pro-neutrality" or even mildly pro-Fascist stance as an act of revenge against England, O'Brien observed: "If, as they tell us, Great Britain is practically dead, of what use would our isolation be to us if the world was ruled by Hitlerism or Communism?"

Life went on as usual in most respects. *The Cambrian* announced that the Lloyd Junge family were the recipient of "an old-time Thanksgiving gift"—a 7-pound, 14-ounce baby girl named Marilyn Louise on November 27.

An advertisement for the Camo Theatre noted that *One Night In Lisbon*, with Madeline Carroll and Fred MacMurray, would be playing two nights in Cambria. Admission was 39 cents for adults and 17 cents for children, "including tax."

And radio listeners were reminded that A.P. Giannini, founder of Bank of America, would speak to California over the Don Lee Network on Tuesday, December 9, from 6:30 to 7 p.m.

The North Coast was about to lose an important connection with its past. Emma Jane Leffingwell, born in Massachusetts in 1849, lay dying at the home of her daughter, Lena Sanders of San Luis Obispo.

And so life went on.

On that Saturday evening, local residents went to the final showings of *The Maltese Falcon* at the Obispo Theatre.

The next morning in the newspapers there were reports of the USC-UCLA football game, and sports fans listened to the Mutual Broadcasting System's broadcast of a professional football game from New York's Polo Grounds.

Shortly before 11:30 a.m. that Sunday, Len Sterling, the staff announcer for Mutual, broke into the broadcast with this Associated Press report: "Flash—Washington—White House Says Japs Attack Pearl Harbor." This bulletin was heard by listeners to San Luis Obispo's Radio Station KVEC (for Valley Electric Company).

NBC continued playing a Sammy Kaye serenade, and CBS played some studio orchestra music, preferring to await further bulletins for its regularly scheduled 11:30 news program.

That news arrived shortly in this form:

San Luis Obispo Mayor Fred Kimball during a radio station KVEC broadcast featuring a military band. *Photo courtesy of San Luis Obispo County Historical Museum.*

"Washington, December 7 (AP)—President Roosevelt said in a statement today that the Japanese had attacked Pearl Harbor, Hawaii, from the air.

"The attack of the Japanese also was made on all naval and military 'activities' on the island of Oahu."

That evening, the *Telegram-Tribune* published a special edition with incredible speed. Details were still scanty concerning the events at Oahu. Premature rumors of a Japanese air strike and landings on the Philippines also were reported. But the war was brought home to the Central Coast with an urgent request: "Please Go Easy On Phone Calls!"

Radio stations throughout the Pacific States had gone off the air to prevent their being used as guide beacons for Japanese aircraft. General William O. Ryan of the 4th Interceptor Command ordered all 50 aircraft observation posts in our county to be manned on a 24-hour basis.

A sense of vulnerability was revealed in this newspaper headline: "Oil Storage Centers Protected."

Sheriff's deputies and Union Oil company guards established a watch at the company's tank farm at the southern San Luis Obispo city limits, and steps were taken to protect other valuable oil storage centers from possible sabotage. Sheriff Murray C. Hathaway said roads leading to the tank farm had been closed to traffic. He also reported the oil companies had established their own security measures at Avila Beach and Estero Bay, where until the past three months Japanese tankers had been loading oil.

These actions were taken because the oil lines and oil storage and pumping facilities in the county could be targets of saboteurs who would have complete knowledge of their location, size and value.

It also was revealed that representatives of the sheriff's and district attorney's offices and the oil companies had met to plan security measures in the event of trouble with Japan.

This story first appeared in the San Luis Obispo County Telegram-Tribune.

Part 4

THE WAR HITS HOME

U.S. FUNDS GAVE SHOT IN ARM TO COUNTY

The financial impact of World War II on San Luis Obispo County began before the start of hostilities and involved much more than serving as a site for the training of men at arms.

Federal dollars flowed in through grants authorized by President Franklin D. Roosevelt.

In a front page story on October 3, 1941, the *Telegram-Tribune* reported: "FDR has approved defense public works projects, including a water works project for the City of San Luis Obispo, a water works project for the City of Paso Robles and a county sewer project at San Miguel."

That report also noted a grant for a recreation building for Paso Robles. This may have been to provide a facility for a USO center to serve soldiers at Camp Roberts. The article noted that the water works project for San Luis was in addition to funds that had been approved earlier.

Then on October 6, the newspaper reported that FDR had approved funds for the construction of a county "health center, which is across Johnson Avenue from the General Hospital" in San Luis.

There was more to come. On January 13, 1942, the newspaper disclosed that the Civil Air Authority had approved federal funds for the construction of an airport at San Luis. County Supervisor Richard L. Willett was credited with being the chief advocate for the project under which the county would provide the land.

Then, in what is believed to be the first in a series of such grants, came federal funds for the schools. On Page 1 of its March 4, 1942, edition, the *Telegram-Tribune* reported that Federal School Grants of $78,000 had been approved.

—Stan Harth
La Vista, Vol. 4, No. 2

Warren Groshong

THIS SLO NAVY VETERAN WON'T FORGET PEARL HARBOR

Theres's bound to be some talk about bombs bursting tonight.

About 24 survivors of the December 7, 1941, devastation of Pearl Harbor will meet at 7 p.m. for dinner at the Madonna Inn.

"We always try to meet on the Saturday closest to December 7," said Donald J. "Dutch" Van Harreveld.

"We also have meetings every other month. We want to be sure we keep Pearl Harbor in the forefront so people will remember. We don't want to have a disaster like this again," he said.

Van Harreveld, who is superintendent of the northern division pipeline for the Union Oil Co., was on the *USS Cinchona* when warplanes of the Rising Sun arrived at Pearl that Sunday morning.

The net tender was anchored at the mouth of the harbor at Bishop's Point near Hickam Field. It was a ways away from where the big ships were moored.

"We noticed some big mounds of dirt going up in the air on the north end of Ford Island," said Van Harreveld, who was on deck waiting to raise the ship's colors.

"A few minutes later a two-seater with a big Rising Sun (Japan's insignia) on it flew toward us. The rear gunner fired at us.

"I ran down to the berthing area and told everybody to get up. They were upset with me for trying to wake them up.

"Then a bomb dropped a couple of hundred feet from the ship. And I ended up being the last one to get back on deck. They tried to crawl right over me."

The rest is history.

The next day, the United States declared war on Japan.

"I count my blessings every day," said Van Harreveld, "that I was one of those who survived."

This article first appeared in the December 8, 1979, issue of the San Luis Obispo County Telegram-Tribune.

Barbara Parker Citlau

RUMBLE OF TRUCKS SIGNALED GOODBYE

George and Barbara Citlau while he was with the 40th Infantry at Camp San Luis. *Photo courtesy of the Citlaus.*

George Citlau and I met at a servicemen's dance at Camp San Luis Obispo in September of 1941.

We dated on weekends. There weren't many places to go out in San Luis Obispo at that time: the Elmo or Obispo theaters for movies; some respectable lounges for dancing like Paul Perrot's, which was where Blondie's Cafe is now; the bowling alley which was on Santa Rosa Street between Marsh and Higuera Streets, and the servicemen's club on the base.

Since I worked in the camp utilities office at Camp San Luis, I had a sticker on my folks' car that enabled me to pass through the entrance gate without having to stop.

On Sunday morning, December 7, 1941, I was washing my hair, getting ready to go to a movie later that day with George, when "Ferdinand" bellowed and bellowed. "Ferdinand" was a very loud horn atop the fire house that was sounded at noon and also used as the city's fire alarm. This time the sound was so persistent that we turned on the radio and heard the news of the attack on Pearl Harbor.

I hurriedly dried my hair and asked my father if I could take the car to drive out to the camp and see George. He agreed, and away I went. Since I had the sticker on the car's windshield, the sentry waved me through, thinking I was called to work in the emergency.

George, who was in Company B of the 115th Engineers of the 40th Infantry Division, wrote the following that day: "I was in the latrine shaving when 'Hislop' came in and said war was declared. He was excited and wild-eyed. I thought he was drunk as I didn't know what he was talking about. That took care of the date I had that afternoon. Here's hoping everything goes OK."

PAUL PERROT'S
GRILL AND BUVETTE

SAN LUIS OBISPO,
CALIFORNIA

George Citlau and Barbara Parker enjoyed time together at Paul Perrot's Grill and Bar (1020 Morro Street) and Buvette (1011 Higuera Street). *Postcard view courtesy of San Luis Obispo County Historical Museum.*

I drove to George's encampment which was where the California Men's Colony now is and stayed there until I was told to leave. We ate in the Post Exchange.

The next morning I went to work early and got to see George for a few minutes before I had to be in the office at 8 o'clock. Then at noon I drove over to his outfit during my lunch break and was able to contact him to say hello. After work I returned there to see and talk with him again. The soldiers were on alert, standing by for orders.

Sometime during the night of December 8, I heard a lot of army trucks rumbling past my parents' home on Broad Street. There was a blackout, and the convoys were driving out Highway 227 to Arroyo Grande before getting on to Highway 101.

The next morning when I went to work I drove to George's quarters. But that had been George's outfit rolling out Broad Street in the dark of the previous night, leaving Camp San Luis.

WARTIME HUMOR

"And did you make these biscuits with your own little hands?" inquired the Sarge.

"Yes," said the new baker. "Why?"

"Oh, nothin'," murmured the Sarge. "I was just wonderin' who helped you lift 'em off the stove."

—*SHOT 'N SHELL*, May 6, 1942

Patrick C. Brown

NIGHT WATCH IN AVILA PROVED DISCONCERTING

Patrick Brown, the lonely guard.
Photo courtesy of Patrick Brown.

At 2 a.m. the shiploading crew was sitting on the warm pipeline on the dock at Port San Luis and keeping an eye on a Union Oil tanker, the *Montebello*, taking on a load of crude oil. Little did we anticipate the world-shaking events we would witness in the days ahead.

The open doors to the well-lighted entrance to the officers' quarters looked warm and inviting to us tired souls who were working a 12-hour shift with little sleep. We had another tanker waiting to load in Berth 5 on the west side of the dock and another empty tanker in the bay. The wharf and all the ships were lighted like jewels in those early hours of December 7, 1941. If the Japanese-Americans had been bent on sabotage, as so many suspected in the frantic days which were to follow, they could have destroyed the ships and shore installations several hours before the attack on Pearl Harbor.

After a light breakfast and a day of fitful sleep on December 7, I learned upon arising about Pearl Harbor.

The Avila area was in the grip of quiet anxiety as I arrived at the oil wharf that night. All the ships were at anchor in the bay, and we of the wharf crew were assigned different stations from which to watch for trespassers and possible saboteurs. I was given a three-quarter-inch by 24-inch iron bolt and told to stand guard at the wharf gate. After standing there for awhile, I realized I was directly under an overhead light. While I couldn't see more than 25 feet around me, others could see me for several hundred feet. So I took my iron bolt and went up the wharf into the darkness where I almost froze.

The night of December 8th was a different story. Avila was alive with soldiers from the army camps, and I was stopped several times before I arrived at the Union Oil wharf. Our lunch and smoking room had been taken over by the soldiers, and little tents and machine gun emplacements dotted

The Union Oil wharf at Avila, where Patrick Brown stood guard with a most unusual weapon. *Photo courtesy of the San Luis Obispo County Historical Museum.*

the end of the wharf. Several times during the night, all hands were called out so that everyone would be ready for a possible invasion.

For about two weeks, the Avila loading terminal was shut down. No ships could leave—and their crews were not very anxious to leave anyway. The first ship to finally leave was the *Montebello,* headed north. Near Cambria, a Japanese submarine sank it.

We soon started loading ships again but under almost total "blackout" conditions. In order to pick up the mooring lines from the ship, the tug had to search for it in the dark. Then when we faintly saw a huge, upright, black mountain ahead of us, we would use a small flashlight to locate the mooring line dangling from the ship for us to take. If the light was on much more than an instant, the telephone would ring on the dock and the Army would tell us to "get that d_____ light off" or they would "shoot it out."

It wasn't long before the oil installation at Avila was painted a flat, camouflage color which made it far less visible from the ocean. As the war continued, we became used to seeing the drab tankers arriving and leaving, armed with their Navy gun crews, cannons, machine guns and degaussing (demagnetizing) booms.

Many times when I was alone on the dock as the war dragged along, I would look into the blinding glare of the setting sun and wonder if an enemy submarine could be sitting on the other side of the breakwater, taking a bead on us.

This article first appeared in Vol. 4, No. 2 of La Vista: The Journal of Central Coast History.

HE LEARNED
WHY MOTORISTS STARED

My Japanese rancher asked me on Saturday, December 6, 1941, if I would work for him on Sunday to help harvest his lettuce crop for the Monday market.

My job was to distribute the crates in the field and put a paper lining in each crate. The Japanese men cut the lettuce heads off, trimmed them, folded the paper over the top and nailed a lid on each crate. When the truck came, I helped load it.

On Sunday, we worked straight through from 10 o'clock in the morning until 3 o'clock in the afternoon, and it wasn't until I got home that I learned the Japanese had bombed Pearl Harbor and that the United States was at war with Japan.

I then realized why so many people had stopped their cars and just stared at us.

When the rancher came to my house to pay me, he paid me double wages and said, "Pretty bad. Maybe one day everything go."

—Bill Froom
La Vista, Vol. 4, No. 2

GAS LIGHTS ONCE
WERE A CLAIM TO FAME

In 1940 when I came to San Luis Obispo, many streets were unpaved and without street signs. The city still had gas street lights. As a matter of fact, San Luis Obispo was mentioned in Ripley's Believe It Or Not as a city where young men rode their bicycles around town each night to light the gas street lights. Charles Cattaneo was one of these young men.

Everyone knew something was about to explode but did not know when, how or why. Camp San Luis Obispo was being built quickly and seemingly without much regulation.

—Ethel G. Cooley
La Vista, Vol. 4, No. 2

Mark Hall-Patton

DECEMBER 7TH BIRTHDAY GIRL RECALLS BAD SURPRISE

It was Frances McElhinney's birthday. She and her family were in the Huasna area, where they raised hay for their horse on the Burnett Reeves ranch. Having been out on the ranch all day, the family had not been listening to the radio.

That evening Frances and her family started back to San Luis Obispo. They passed an unusually large number of military trucks on their way. Frances commented on this when they stopped at the Waldorf Cafe on Pomeroy in Pismo Beach. Their waitress told them about the attack on Pearl Harbor; this was their first knowledge of the event. Quite a birthday surprise.

On Christmas Day of 1941, Frances and her family went to Shell Beach. Driving down the highway, they were aware of the preparations for war but did not see anything out of the ordinary along their route on Highway 101.

The family spent the day with friends, the Carters, who lived in Shell Beach. They went clamming, then the visit continued into the evening.

It was a "dim out" night, so they could not have their car's headlights on as they traveled home on Highway 101. Only the use of parking lights was allowed. As they slowly drove up the south side of Ontario Grade, which at that time rose rather steeply out of today's Sunset Palisades, and just before they reached the Avila Road turnout, they suffered a shock.

Seemingly out of nowhere, a field artillery piece loomed next to the road, its barrel appearing to reach out over the highway. To say this was startling is an understatement. The gun had not been there earlier in the day, apparently having been moved in under cover of darkness.

The gun was later placed in the graded area still visible above the highway at that site. It was well camouflaged and stood there throughout the war. Frances recalls always noticing it when she visited friends in the South County, because it always reminded her of that Christmas night.

WARTIME INTEREST

...we'll toss in a bouquet of G.I. flowers to the Fort Ord *Panorama!* The *Panorama* it was which dreamed up "Zip Your Lip!" and started the ball rolling on that catchy and important phrase. —*SHOT 'N SHELL*, May 27, 1942

Pauline Bradley Dubin

KIYOMI, WHERE ARE YOU?

Kiyomi with Paul and Mary Ann Dubin in March, 1942. *Photo courtesy of Pauline Dubin.*

It was Monday morning, the day after Pearl Harbor. My Japanese-American nursemaid stood outside the glass-paned kitchen door, her head down, her lips quivering. Ordinarily, Kiyomi let herself in with her own key.

I opened the door and took her into my arms and consoled her by murmuring, "It's not your fault, Kiyomi." We both cried a little.

Kiyomi came to work for us after graduating from high school. She wanted to earn money for college. And her parents wanted her to live with a Caucasian family to improve her understanding of American ways.

She lived with us, but on weekends she went home to her family in Arroyo Grande. Her sister, Hiroko, had a similar domestic position, but Hiroko was promptly fired after Pearl Harbor.

Kiyomi was a joy to have around. She was a great help to our family. I was able to get away some afternoons for shopping, and I felt perfectly secure in leaving my 4-year-old Mary Ann with her.

I can still picture the two of them, sitting on the front steps and waving to me as I boarded the little green bus that stopped in front of our home on Mitchell Drive.

A real test of Kiyomi's dependability came one night when a blackout occurred after Harry and I had left with our two older boys, Charles and Paul, for a community concert.

During the concert, the senior high school where the violinist was performing was suddenly plunged into darkness. An audible gasp swelled up in the auditorium, and you could almost hear hearts pounding. The music went on, for the violinist had a blue light which shone on his music.

It was an eerie moment. We immediately thought of our little girl at home and of the rumors about our town being a target for bombing because of the proximity of Camp San Luis.

"Let's get home," Harry whispered. So, the four of us tiptoed down from the balcony and went out to the parking lot to find our car in the dark. Driving the car without headlights was a strain, for other cars were driving in the dark, too. We made the trip home safely. There in the living room, in the rocking chair, were Kiyomi and Mary Ann, talking and wondering about the strange noises outside.

The relocation of the Japanese people away from the Pacific Coast was a sad and touchy topic. Radio commentators hammered away at stories about likely sabotage. I remember Fulton Lewis Jr. was especially persistent. When he came on, we huddled around the radio. But Kiyomi would disappear.

We all shared her anguish at the very thought of internment. It was called relocation. But we couldn't believe that it would happen here. Not in our country. When it did, Kiyomi accepted it with true stoicism.

She had to console me when I railed at the unfairness of it all.

"Don't you worry," Kiyomi said, "we'll be back when the war is over."

We corresponded for awhile. Then my new baby, my red-haired Michael, came into the picture, and our letters gradually faded away.

We've often wondered about Kiyomi. Did she and her family ever come back to California? Did she ever go to college?

Kiyomi, where are you?

Pauline Dubin later located "Kiyomi," who asked her to use a pseudonym. This story originally appeared in La Vista, *Vol. 4, No. 2.*

WARTIME HUMOR

At last Thursday's Jewish Seder observance, at which Major General Simpson and Colonel Bull were guests, a soldier walked up to the Camp Commander.

With proper aplomb, he reached deep into his G.I. hip pocket and pulled out a badly battered cigar. "Colonel, for you, Sir—from the boys," were his faltering words.

The Colonel awaited further comment, but the blushing soldier remained rigid.

"Son, don't you think you should tell me your outfit, so I'll know to whom I am indebted for this fine cigar?" questioned Colonel Bull.

"Uh-uh!! I can't do that. It's a military secret," said the soldier.

"But, I'd like to know who made the presentation. What's your outfit?" repeated the Camp Commander.

Whereupon a lieutenant stepped in to assist with, "It's the Colonel, soldier—tell him!"

The soldier, lip-zipped to the end said—

"Nope! Not me. He may not be what he seems."

—*SHOT 'N SHELL*, April 8, 1942

Liz Krieger

WE WERE AMERICANS, TOO

Paul Piantanida, a son of Italian immigrants, suffered taunts in San Luis Obispo. He helped liberate Buchenwald. *Photo courtesy of Bill Cattaneo.*

"**W**op!" "Damn Dago!" Paul Piantanida's memory still rings with the epithets hurled at him across the playgrounds at Emerson, Hawthorne and Court Schools, and later at the old San Luis Jr. High at the corner of Marsh and Johnson. Being Italian-American, with parents from the old country, wasn't easy for Paul, whose nephew, Bill Cattaneo, broadcasts popular historical vignettes of "Our Town" daily over radio station KVEC.

"I was in more battles as a youngster and always had to be ready to fight. I didn't want to be mean, but it was as if some kids wanted to make you that way with their taunts," Piantanida muses.

"We lived on the wrong side of the tracks, south of Broad and South Streets where the Pacific Coast Railroad used to cross. Most of us were Italian, Portuguese, Mexican, Japanese or Chinese. We all came in for a lot of name calling," he believes. "I had some good teachers, but there wasn't much they could do" about prejudice.

When I asked Piantanida, who lives in Oregon, what Italian immigrants and their American-born children thought of Mussolini in San Luis Obispo, he unhesitatingly exclaimed, "Most were sympathetic to Mussolini before World War II. We liked his building highways, schools, draining lakes and marshes for farmland.If people are honest, they will admit that many approved of" the Italian leader who was an ally of Hitler.

Marlene Piuma Souza, however, remembers her mother, also the child of Italian immigrants, as being critical of Mussolini. "She said he was such a show-off!"

Marlene was lucky. She was not subjected to anti-Italian sentiments at Mission School in San Luis, which was run by the Immaculate Heart sisters.

After Pearl Harbor, the coast of California from Monterey County to the Oregon border saw the forced relocation and restriction of many Italian immigrants who had not gotten their final U.S. naturalization papers. Some

Jack Lohrberg, a son of a German immigrant, and his bride, Nina, who was a Navy WAVE. *Photo courtesy of Jack Lohrberg.*

families had to move a few miles inland. Some lost jobs when they were forbidden to travel near the coast. Some youngsters lost a year of high school, as they were unable to reach their schools. Stephen Fox presents hundreds of poignant interviews about their plight in his 1990 book, *The Unknown Internment.*

However, in San Luis Obispo County, Italian "enemy aliens," as they were called by the U.S. government, fared much better. Neither Paul Piantanida nor Marlene Souza knew of any who were forcibly relocated. Neither knew of any Italians in the county who were persecuted by their neighbors or employers because we were now at war with Mussolini's Italy.

San Luis Obispo, like America itself, was not a perfect society in the 1930s. Residents of varying ethnic backgrounds didn't always get along. But they innately knew that whatever their grievances, this was the best act going. And so they stood up to defend their country in its hour of greatest peril.

Paul would volunteer for the U.S. Army and survive the Battle of the Bulge. And as a member of a tank unit under General George Patton, he would help liberate Buchenwald, a Nazi concentration camp in which people died because they were considered "different."

Paul's brother, Phillip, decided to join the Marines. War in the Pacific would leave shrapnel in his brain and the left side of his body permanently paralyzed.

Paul's neighbor, Jack Lohrberg, was a sophomore in high school when his family moved to San Luis Obispo. Jack has no memories of meanness over his German name. "Obviously," he says, "there were undercurrents of alarm" over the Nazi build-up in Europe.

Jack's father had migrated from Germany about 1908. World War I saw him working in the shipyards of San Francisco.

Even though Mr. Lohrberg was nostalgic for "the Fatherland," he did not discourage Jack from enlisting in the Marines in March, 1939. "The depression was still going strong, there were big layoffs at Union Oil where I worked, so I thought I might as well go in the service," Jack recalls. "I wasn't being patriotic or anything."

Still, Jack managed to give eight years to the Marines, serving in the South Pacific. He did find time to marry a pretty WAVE, Nina, in 1945. Besides his wife, the service gave him another bonus, the G.I. Bill which paid for him to complete his mechanical engineering degree at Cal Poly, which had been an interrupted dream during the thirties.

Turn the calendar back to the year of our battle for Independence—1776. That was 166 years ago, and these six colored soldiers have that much accumulative service in the United States Army. Standing beside an old caisson are, left to right, Sergeant John Speed, 32 years of service; First Sergeant Troy Berrin, 23; Tech. 5th George Dulin, 25, and Tech. 5th Erwin Waterhouse, 26. Aboard the ancient artillery vehicle are Sergeant James Beasley, 31, and Tech. Sgt. Dennis Dyes, 29. The caisson is purely effect for photographic purposes, since most of these old timers spent their time in the Infantry. —*Photo by Lennie, official Camp San Luis Obispo photographer* SHOT 'N SHELL, *April 27, 1942*

Joyce Mathison Carscaden

THE TRIP HOME ON DECEMBER 7 ENDED IN SAD SIGHT

On December 7, 1941, I was living with the Villa family in San Luis Obispo and working for the County Health Department. My family resided four miles north of Cambria at San Simeon Creek on the Van Gorden family farm. On Sundays, my father would make the round trip to San Luis Obispo so that I could spend time with my parents.

That Sunday, my father told me about the attack on Pearl Harbor. I recall asking him, "What does that mean?" He told me that it meant war. At the age of 20, I had little understanding of what the war would mean to us.

When we returned to San Luis Obispo in the early evening, I was amazed to see people clustered on the outside of the fence bordering Camp San Luis Obispo. They were talking to their loved ones on the inside of the fence, reaching through to touch one another and to say goodbye. I realized then that families would be torn apart.

The public health officer for whom I began working in June of 1941 was a Dr. Bingham, who soon was called into the Navy. For many months, a physician drove down from San Francisco to hold the department's clinics. Later the United States Public Health Service supplied Dr. Philip Bearg, who stayed for the duration of the war.

Due to Camp San Luis Obispo, the health department was confronted with considerable extra work. The government set up an emergency maternity fund to pay for the care of servicemen's wives who were having babies. And the influx of so many men into the community caused the creation of a venereal disease investigation, treatment and control section. Ours was a two-person office. The other woman was in charge of vital statistics, so the rest of the work fell to me. After a few weeks, two additional positions were added to cover these new programs.

Because of fear of invasion along the coast, my family had to maintain total black-out conditions. The Coast Guard constantly patrolled the area in trucks. When civilians drove their cars after dark, the vehicles' lights were never turned on. A Coast Guard truck would be driven ahead of my mother's car so she could attend meetings of her lodge after dark. Because Cambria at that time was a very small village, the military personnel became a part of the community, and many men were "adopted" by the families there.

As a USO hostess, I met young men from throughout the nation and danced the equivalent of many miles, wearing out precious shoes that only could be obtained with ration stamps. Nylons were a luxury. Mostly we wore rayon hose which bagged terribly at the knees and ankles. Once three pairs of my hose were stolen after I hung them on an outside line to dry after I had washed them.

We all lost friends and acquaintances in that war. But we also made new friends from all over the country who remain correspondents with us and keep in touch even today after all these years have passed.

The old fire station and City Hall in San Luis Obispo, with "Ferdinand" in the bell tower. *Photo courtesy of Bill Callaway.*

Elliot Curry

THE NIGHT THE LIGHTS WENT OUT IN SAN LUIS

On the night of December 10, 1941, Mayor Fred C. Kimball stood on Radio Peak just north of the city and watched the lights go out.

In less than a minute, San Luis Obispo looked like this:

It was only three days after the Japanese attack on Pearl Harbor, but already San Luis Obispo was on a wartime footing. The blackout had been ordered by the Pacific Coast Interceptor Command as the armed forces took precautions against the expected air attack.

December 7 was on a Sunday that year. Anyone who experienced the shock of that day is not likely to forget it.

To San Luis Obispo, the declaration of war had a special significance. Camp San Luis Obispo, originally a National Guard encampment, had already been greatly expanded and the 40th Division was mobilized and in training here.

The day the bombs fell on Pearl Harbor, guards were immediately put on alert at the city water reservoirs, at the Union Oil tank farm and at city and county buildings.

Trenches were dug at strategic points overlooking potential beach landing sites. Some of the old, sand-bagged fortifications could still be seen long after the war was over.

On the day before the first blackout test, Mayor Kimball announced that it would be signaled by five short blasts on the city fire horn. The horn, mounted on the old city hall on Higuera Street, was known to deafened residents as "Ferdinand."

At the same time, there would be a quick dimming of city street lights, warning motorists to pull to the curb at once and turn out their cars' lights.

In those mad days, many feared that western civilization might be going into a blackout.

The end of the old fire station. *Photo courtesy of Bill Callaway.*

Before the victory was won, some 500,000 American troops would pass through Camp San Luis Obispo for division training. Nine divisions were in that historic passage.

San Luis Obispo would never turn back. The little city that Mayor Kimball looked down upon that winter night would never be the same again.

Reprinted from the Telegram-Tribune, *December 10, 1975.*

Walter Tanaka

"MOST LONELY YEARS" HIT SOLDIER AT CAMP ROBERTS

Walter Tanaka received his basic training at Camp Roberts. *Photo courtesy of San Luis Obispo County Historical Museum.*

I was graduated from San Luis Obispo High School in June of 1940, and while I dreamed that I might be able to go to college, I knew that in the aftermath of the Great Depression there was no possibility.

My family needed every hand to work on the land we leased from Mr. Pereira of the Round Dairy Farm south of San Luis along old Highway 101.

The house we lived in was set back on the property near the bank of SLO creek. It was the former home of Horace Ainsley Vachell, a turn-of-the-century poet. The house had five fireplaces and a hallway long enough for my young sister to skate on. With high ceilings and lots of windows, it was drafty and cold in the winter. We split a lot of firewood to try to keep warm.

On October 16, 1940, I registered for the Army draft. My registration number was #15, and my draft number was #5368. On June 2, 1941, I was drafted and went for a physical exam at the National Guard Armory in San Francisco. My reception center was the Presidio of Monterey. I arrived there on June 4. On June 7, I was transferred to Camp Roberts to receive basic training in infantry, specializing in heavy weapons.

Here are some of my recollections:

• Our dress uniform consisted of khakis with tie and felt campaign hat.

• When training, we wore blue denims, denim floppy hats and canvas leggings.

• We took pride in being heavy weapons men and took pictures with 30-caliber machine gun belts loaded with ammunition draped around our necks.

• I prided myself on my dexterity in gun drill. A fellow recruit and I were the fastest team in the company in moving forward with the machine gun barrel and tripod and setting up and loading the weapon.

• The temperature at Camp Roberts during the summer would rise to 110 to 115 degrees Fahrenheit. We went on road marches as far as 20 miles.

Walter Tanaka, right, joins a buddy in wearing ammunition belts for 30-caliber machine guns while training at Camp Roberts. *Photo courtesy of Walter Tanaka.*

The platoon leader would stand our platoon in ranks prior to a march and require us to swallow salt tablets with water from our canteens. This gave some of us stomach cramps.

• We trained with machine guns on a 1,000-inch range, learning to traverse, depress, elevate and bracket into the target, firing for accuracy. A cloud of dust would rise when all the guns fired.

• When we had rest stops during marches, we had our share of horse play. Wayne B. Copley of King City, one of the recruits in our platoon, got his feet tied to the trunk of a tree after he climbed it.

• True to Army life, we had to shine our shoes, sweep and mop the floors, make our beds and line up our cots and footlockers.

During our eight weeks of training, there was an outbreak of measles and mumps in our company. Everywhere our company went, a flag bearer carried a yellow flag before us. We were quarantined from the Post Exchange and confined to our company area.

In those basic training days, I was just another American GI who received his Army indoctrination and training without fuss or fanfare and without any questions regarding my loyalty to my country, the United States of America.

After basic training at Camp Roberts, I was transferred to Company H, 17th Infantry Regiment, 7th Division at Ford Ord.

Then, on December 7, 1941, the terrible tragedy of Pearl Harbor and war between the United States and Japan took place. Public opinion, fanned by the press, changed everything. We Japanese-Americans (*Nisei*) were suspect purely at face value.

The most lonely years of my life followed—years during which many of my fellow Americans with whom I grew up in San Luis Obispo were no longer ready to accept me as one of them.

WARTIME HUMOR

What the five cent cigar needs is a good country.

—*SHOT 'N SHELL*, May 13, 1942

Hilda J. Roza

TONY PAID HIGH PRICE FOR SHIELDING BROTHER

Tony and Hilda Roza on their engagement day. *Photo courtesy of Hilda Roza.*

My maiden name was Hilda J. Quartilho, and at the age of nearly 7 my mother brought me from Terceira, one of the Azores Islands belonging to Portugal, to join my father in San Luis Obispo.

When I was 19 years old, I became engaged to Tony F. Roza Jr., the eldest of three sons of A.F. Roza Sr., who at one time grew sweet peas for the Burpee Seed Company in what is now part of the Laguna Lake residential and commercial area. Tony had been a track star and played baseball and football in high school. He was 24 years old when we became engaged.

The military draft had begun, and Louis F. Roza, the middle of the three brothers, was called up. Because of the draft numbering system used in those days, Henry F. Roza, the younger brother, would be next. Because Henry still lived at home and was of special concern to his mother, Tony talked with me about the possibility of his trading places with his younger brother on the draft list. This was possible under a recently enacted law that stated that not more than two siblings from each set of parents could be drafted. And such a trade would mean that Henry would not be drafted. We decided to do it, thinking that it was best for Henry and that the one year of active service the draft called for would give us time to plan our wedding.

On November 11, 1941, Tony was inducted into the Army. In those days, November 11th was known as Armistice Day, marking the end of World War I. With the December 7, 1941, attack on Pearl Harbor, Tony's one year of service was extended to "the duration of the war." He was sent to Fort Leonard Wood in Missouri for basic training. There he suffered frost bite so severely that he couldn't walk. After he recovered, he was sent back out into the snow.

Tony was assigned to the 27th Infantry Division, which was comprised mostly of soldiers from New York State and which was the first complete division to be deployed in the Pacific theater of operations. The division's initial destination was Pearl Harbor. Tony said it took three weeks to get there from the West Coast because the troop ships were repeatedly turned back by the threat of Japanese submarines. When they arrived, he said, fires were still smoldering at Pearl Harbor.

After serving as a private, then heavy truck driver in the 102nd Combat Engineers, Tony became a construction foreman. He took part in the invasions of Saipan, Kwajalein and Okinawa. The following is from a commendation Tony received for his actions on Okinawa:

"On the 17th April 1945 at about 2000 hours Tec 4 Roza was part of a seven man detail assigned to me to deliver five M-2 Assault Boats under the cover of darkness to the 106th Infantry in their front line positions. While loading these boats on a truck at our Motor Pool the enemy began laying down a heavy artillery barrage with shells exploding 50 to 100 yards away which forced the detail to take cover several times only to return and continue towards the completion of the mission. In delivering the boats to the front lines it was necessary to travel through an open field and although the infantry had been ordered to send up no flares, three or four flares were sent up which resulted in the complete illumination of the open field. Although under direct observation of the enemy the detail delivered the boats.... "

During the war I was active in doing what I could for the effort, including serving as secretary for the V-12 cadet program at Cal Poly, helping soldiers enroll for their military insurance at Camp San Luis Obispo and, later, working as a stenographer at camp headquarters. I also was active with the USO as a hostess, teaching some of the soldiers to dance and serving cake and cookies. During the last part of the war I became chief secretary for District Attorney H. C. Grundell.

When the war ended, Tony was eligible for discharge but the Army considered him "necessary to the battlefield" and he wasn't discharged until October 17, 1945, at Camp Beale, California. We were reunited in San Jose. Then on November 11, 1945, exactly four years after he was inducted, we were married in the Old Mission Church in a white formal (happy) ceremony. Our wedding barbecue was at the former Portuguese I.D.E.S. Hall on Mill Street.

In not quite ten years, Tony died on October 27, 1955, at the Veterans Administration Hospital in Fresno as a result, we believe, of service-connected medical problems, including the severe frostbite he suffered during basic training. During his long illness, one leg had to be amputated, and his remaining foot had become gangrenous. Because his military medical records had been lost, we were unable to substantiate our claim.

Tony was 40 years old when he died. We had a daughter, Judy Lynn, during our too short ten years together.

Wickson R. Woolpert

PRE-LAW STUDENT AWOKE TO NAVY'S CALL TO DUTY

On Pearl Harbor Day, December 7, 1941, I was a pre-law student at the University of California, Berkeley. Having joined the Navy's Merchant Marine Reserve to "safely" attend college, I received word by telephone of the bombing and was instructed to report to the Treasure Island Naval Facility "tomorrow." I did.

The next few days found me, a Seaman First Class because of my Merchant Marine background, in the confusion of Treasure Island. My clearest memory of those days is of a dark night, sirens wailing and the lights on the bridge being turned off. The word was that a Japanese air attack was underway—a false but chilling report. I suspect the motorists on the bridge were more frightened than our confused, just-assembled group of naval personnel.

By Christmas I had been sent alone to an Alameda shipyard to guard a purse seiner fishing boat the Navy had conscripted from its owners. The only food left on board was a bag of large, brown onions which, when boiled, were fairly good under the conditions. I have fond memories of a dockside restaurant which served good dinners for 35 cents.

By early January of 1942 I was taken, with several other seamen and an officer, by truck to Avila—as it was then called.

Why Avila? We were informed while driving south on Highway 101: It was clear the Japanese naval forces were substantial and an attack on the Pacific Coast was likely. A submarine had shelled the coast north of Santa Barbara and one Union Oil tanker had been sunk off Cambria. The Navy had not prepared for its ships to be along the Pacific Coast. Much more logically, the fleet moved between strategic locations in the Western Pacific. Because of the losses at Pearl Harbor, no US naval force would be moved to the California coast in the future. Therefore, we were it.

What was "it?" Simply described, we were to operate yachts taken from private owners and fishing boats of the kind so often seen in the coastal waters. Would we throw rocks, or use rifles? Obviously, neither. Instead, we would have machine guns and depth charges, or "ash cans." This did not mean that we would have our small boats equipped with propulsion devices which would toss the depth charges far beyond the boats. Such a propulsion device probably would overturn a boat. Instead, those craft that could be were equipped with ramps, metal sloping runways. If we came upon a Japanese submarine, we were to let the depth charges roll down the sloping rack off the stern. When deep enough in the sea, the charges would explode with great force.

Even simple seamen could understand that. But one of the unsolved mysteries of some concern to us was what would happen to such a slow boat once the ash cans had been dropped? The explosion would be within seconds. Would the blast destroy not only the submarine but also our boat — and us? We never were told whether the Navy had tried one of these attacks to determine what would happen.

The Navy had taken over the Yacht Club headquarters at the head of Avila pier. My duty was to share watches on the radio-telephone communication system. It was enviable duty. The only violence I saw while at Avila was twofold: I had brought a bow and arrows with me to be used for hunting, not war. Once while hiking on a hill east of Avila, I came upon a skunk. Although I now know how cruel it was, I took aim and hit the skunk, killing it. Not having many arrows, I pulled out the arrow and went back to the base. When I arrived at the pier, and before even getting in the door of the building, I was confronted by angry friends who insisted my odor was too much for civilized sailors. They combined and collared me, then dragged me out on the pier and unceremoniously dumped me—and my bow and arrows—into the surf.

When I wasn't on duty, the beach was my terrain for body surfing, kicking footballs and girl watching. One day, another sailor and I were running up and down the beach when we saw three very pretty girls sunning near the wall north of the pier. One girl particularly attracted me. By that evening I had arranged a date with her to go bowling in Pismo Beach. Nellouise Torres was "mine." The other girls were Harriet Rivers (now Tripke) of San Luis Obispo and Jessie Kelley, Nellouise's cousin. Later, Jessie enlisted in the Marines and met and married Walter Borg, a fellow Marine.

Nellouise, a "local" whose family can be traced back to Lt. Jose Francisco Ortega, who served under Portolá, was my first real girlfriend. We met on April 28th, became engaged on May 16th and were married on June 14, 1942, at the Presbyterian Church on Marsh Street in San Luis Obispo.

During that time span, we spent most of our working hours to mutual advantage. She was a nighttime long distance telephone operator, and my radio-telephone shift was from midnight to 8 a.m. It was a perfect combination, and between business and Navy calls, we spent many of those hours "just talking" on the telephone.

During the summer and fall of 1942, we had an apartment over the E.E. Long Piano Co. on Marsh Street at Garden Street. When our work du-

Wickson and Nellouise Woolpert during his Navy days. *Photo courtesy of the Woolperts.*

ties conflicted, I found extra time could be spent earning a bit of "pin" money. There was a restaurant across from the Avila pier run by the Schlegels. They were nice, understanding people who didn't mind at all that a sailor boy had learned to beat their pinball machines by bumping and pushing at appropriate times.

Soon the Navy operation was moved to Morro Bay, where the Navy took over a site on a bluff not far from where the Pacific Gas & Electric Co. plant is now located. When not on duty and unable to return to our Marsh Street apartment, I found time to toss a javelin on the beach north of the rock, hoping to return to my place on the U.C. track team.

Of course, the story doesn't end in 1942. There were separations, different duty stations, officer's training and eventually overseas orders. However, before I left for overseas, Charron, our first child, was born in San Luis Obispo.

I saw the war's ending in the far Pacific while serving as a deck officer on a Landing Ship, Tank (LST).

With peace came the work days, college and law school at Berkeley. Finally a choice: Join a law firm in San Francisco, or return to San Luis Obispo?

Fortunately, we made the right choice: San Luis Obispo.

Eleanor Ormonde Craveiro

SLO COED AND FAMILY WATCHED A SAD PARADE

On December 7, 1941, I lived with my parents on a small farm in the area of what is now the 3100 block of South Higuera Street in San Luis Obispo. Our home was set back about 75 feet from what was then Highway 101, the main thoroughfare out of town to the south.

On that memorable day a girl friend of mine and her mother had come to visit. She and I were both engaged to local boys who had been drafted into the Army on November 11, 1941, Armistice Day. They were to train for one year and were to be paid $21 a month.

In those days, as our country was coming out of the Great Depression, very few families had telephones, and we received our information primarily from newspapers and radio broadcasts. In our family, the radio usually was turned on after dinner for a couple of hours if the reception was good; if there was too much static, the radio was turned off.

It was from the radio that we first learned of the attack on Pearl Harbor and of President Franklin D. Roosevelt's plan to go before Congress the next day to ask for a declaration of war. Then we heard an unusually heavy rumbling of trucks passing by on the highway. We rushed out to our front porch and, with tears streaming down our faces, we watched truck after truck pass with young soldiers huddled in the back. They were on their way to guard our coast.

I was attending junior college which was located in the high school. Many of the students were Japanese. The next morning as I boarded the school bus, the driver told me to sit in the seat right behind him. We all were very subdued on our way to school, suffering from shock and apprehension. No conflict arose between the students.

On December 10, 1941, the first black-out drill was conducted throughout California. My recollection is that the instructions were: 1) The city's fire horn will blow three short and one long blasts and street lights will dim; 2) Citizens in their homes will extinguish all lights and proceed to the safest place, preferably a basement; 3) Motorists will steer their vehicles to the curb and extinguish all lights, and 4) Merchants will extinguish neon and other identification signs.

All of this was only a prelude to my becoming my husband's "dog tag" for three and one-half years in faraway towns.

Beverly Bukey Anderson

MOB, SUBMARINE JOLTED PISMO BEACH FIRST GRADER

It can be difficult when you are a first grader attending a school that is new to you, but it can be almost shattering to lose a new friend because of what grownups tell you is an "historical event."

And it can be downright frightening when your mother spots an enemy submarine from your home's picture window.

That's the way it was for me during the first of 1942.

Our family moved to Shell Beach in January of that year, and I was enrolled in Pismo Elementary School. There were so few of us from Shell Beach who attended the school that we younger pupils had to wait for the older ones to complete their school day before boarding the bus for the ride home.

It was while waiting for the bus that I met a Japanese-American girl I will call Suzy.

Suzy's family grew peas and other vegetables in the area of what is now called Sunset Palisades. My mother often would stop to buy produce from them and that would give Suzy and me a little time to play while our mothers talked.

At school, I noticed that some of the children seemed to stay away from Suzy and that my teacher seemed to treat her differently, more coolly than she treated me and others. But Suzy and I were friends, and I didn't care about anything else.

Then one day Suzy was absent, and the teacher told me she would not come back. I was upset and worried and wanted to go to where Suzy lived. When I got home my stepfather was there, and I told him what I had been told about Suzy and of my concern.

He said, "I just came by there. It isn't pretty, but I think you should see. It is an historical event happening in your own town and you'll probably study about it when you are in high school. You might as well know about it first hand."

What I saw when he took me there were people like a flock of locusts going through the fields and knocking down houses and combing through the belongings left behind. Suzy's home was in splintered pieces. I didn't touch anything, not even for a keepsake of my friend Suzy, whose family had been relocated under Executive Order 9066.

Pismo Beach was tranquil in this 1930s scene. *Photo courtesy of San Luis Obispo County Historical Museum.*

Our rented home was just north of the public access to Shell Beach. It was just above the cliff that dropped to the ocean, and the picture window provided a marvelous view.

One morning I heard my mother scream. I got out of bed and ran to her. She was shaking as she closed the drapes across the picture window. We went into the kitchen and, speaking softly so as not to awaken my sleeping baby brother, she said, "I came in the living room like I usually do in the morning and opened the drapes so I could look out at the ocean. This morning as I watched, I saw what looked like something sticking out of the ocean not so far out. Suddenly, a submarine came partially to the surface for a moment and then submerged again."

She took a deep breath and, with tears streaming down her face, added, "It had a big red circle on its side. The enemy is right out there now, and they have seen us. What happens now?"

We were both very frightened, but mother finally decided that the military would handle the situation. And with that I got ready and went off to school.

WARTIME HUMOR

Politician (ending flowery speech to a recent selectee): "You're doing the greatest of all jobs, protecting your country from the ravages of rapacious demagogs (sic). I envy you. I wish I were in your shoes.

Selectee: "Oh, they wouldn't fit you, either."

—SHOT 'N SHELL, April 8, 1942

Cook: "Ever been in the service before?"

K.P.: "Sure, I was a gunner in the navy.

Cook: "Well, start right in shelling these peas."

—SHOT 'N SHELL, April 22, 1942

Lorraine Ludeke Wiech

TEEN LEARNED THAT WAR IS MORE THAN CUTE GI'S

Lorraine Ludeke Wiech in a photo taken when she graduated from Paso Robles High School in 1941. *Photo courtesy of Lorraine Wiech.*

Our family and the Work family of northern San Luis Obispo County had looked forward to Sunday, December 7, 1941, because that was the date for the annual Ludeke-Work December birthday dinner and celebration.

Our families shared a total of six December birthdays.

As I was a college coed, there was a special treat for the 1941 affair, for the Work family had invited four soldiers from Camp Roberts to share in the festivities at their ranch.

We were having a fine time until someone switched on the radio. To us teenage girls, news of the attack on Pearl Harbor was, indeed, bad, but almost as bad were the announcements that the young soldiers were to "report at once" to their units. I must confess that our young men stretched the "at once" order because, after all, they were out at a ranch and could not get back to camp until their hosts transported them.

I believe we girls really did not understand the true magnitude of what had happened. For me, a clearer idea of it came the next morning when I returned to San Luis Obispo Junior College, which at that time was in the high school. The student body was called to an assembly at which one of the administrators discussed the war and concluded by expressing the hope that there would be no incident against any of our Japanese-American classmates. He received a standing ovation for that statement. And I never saw any such incident.

The impact of these events on my life was profound. I remember thinking that, had I not been Caucasian, I might have been "relocated" as some of my classmates were, for my father was a first generation German-American.

IT'S 15 TO 1 THAT VOICE IS HERS!

When you lift the receiver off the hook, the chances are about 15 to 1 that you'll hear the voice of Edith Pavola, Los Angeles. She is one of the many attractive and efficient girls who work at the Camp San Luis Obispo switchboard, in the Signal Office. Long have we wondered what the telephone operators look like, and no longer will it remain one of life's little mysteries. Many is the dogface heart that has been set agallop by a sweet and charming voice, and many are the visions of loveliness that have gripped the imagination when well-modulated and dulcet tones delicately inquire—"Number, please?" Well, the visions weren't foolin'. Miss Pavola gained her training in Los Angeles and came to San Luis Obispo nearly eight months ago.

—*Photo by Lennie*, SHOT 'N SHELL, *June 10, 1942*

Part 5

THE MONTEBELLO SUNK

Helen Bowen Hileman

THE *MONTEBELLO*—
A GIRL'S WONDERLAND

During the late 1930s, my father would go out on the Union Oil tanker *Montebello*, and my mother and I would be allowed to make one trip during the summer when the captain's wife was also aboard. Since passengers were not allowed on tankers, it was necessary to "sign on" as crew members with the seamen's union. I was an "apprentice stewardess," my mother was a "stewardess" and the captain's wife was "nurse." Pay was two cents per month.

My only duties consisted of being "banker" each night for the big Monopoly game in the captain's quarters (Monopoly was the new rage then) and every morning contesting with Captain Andreassen in a lively session of jump rope. I still have the jump rope the crew made for me.

Mid-mornings "Cook" would let me serve up the fresh, hot and spicy cinnamon buns to the crew as he poured mugs of steaming coffee. Tankers always seemed to reach ports on Sundays, in the days when towns were closed up on Sundays, but crew members managed to bring back the Sunday "funnies" for me and a supply of candy bars to last through the return voyage home. "Cook" also would manage to locate a couple of bottles of fresh milk for me.

I dreaded our return to Avila, not only because the voyage was ended, but because the tanker was light and riding high which made the gangplank almost perpendicular to the wharf, a scary descent, and from the ship, the Union Oil wharf looked like a long walk to shore.

The *Montebello*, a Union Oil tanker. *Photo courtesy of San Luis Obispo County Historical Museum.*

Jane H. Bailey

TUGBOAT *ALMA'S* CREW SPENT ANXIOUS NIGHT

Two ships were torpedoed off our coast during the wee hours of December 23, 1941. On the eve of the *Montebello's* ill-fated voyage, those involved in oil storage and shipping knew that the Japanese Emperor's subs were prowling off California.

According to captured official documents detailing in German the data on Japanese submarine activity here, *Sub I-17* chased the Richfield Oil Company ship *Larry Doheny* to the Estero Bay Standard Oil pier (just north of the town of Morro Bay) and almost ashore. A few hours later the Japanese *Sub I-21* pursued and sank the Union Oil Company's *Montebello* off Cambria.

We understand that the captain of the *Montebello* resigned his position at midnight at Avila because he believed that Japanese submarines were offshore and that to proceed was foolhardy. His first mate, Olaf Ekstrom, succeeded him as skipper, to serve only five or six hours before his vessel was sunk and his crew rescued.

On this strange night, Merle Molinari and his Standard Oil service tugboat *Alma* were involved with both the *Doheny* and the *Montebello*. The *Alma* was moored to a buoy just outside Estero Bay.

According to Molinari, "We were alerted that a Standard Oil ship, the *Rheem*, was due to come in and pick up a load of oil. But because of a reported sub in the area, we had been wired orders not to proceed to Estero Bay, but to proceed to the radar buoy and intercept the *Rheem* and warn it to get out of the area."

Molinari continued: "With me were Harold Turri, Vern St. John and the Standard Oil captain, probably Captain Thompson. So we proceeded to the buoy. We tied to it, three miles offshore; a violation of navigation laws, to be sure, but then it was the only thing we could do at night. A bad night: choppy, rough, quite a haze. Couldn't see. After we tied, Harold and I felt we could hear diesel engines cruising on the surface, but we couldn't see anything. So we decided to just stand watch and all sleep but the man on watch.

"At about 3 o'clock Vern came down, awakened me and said, 'I hear shooting but can't see anything.' So I said, 'Well, all we can do is be alert and see what we can see. If anything happens, give us a little call.'

"So I went back to sleep. Well, there wasn't anything to do! At daylight, we decided to return to shore. We'd seen nothing. It was still hazy, and as we approached shore there was a ship anchored inside of us, toward shore. And we said, 'Oh my gosh, the *Rheem's* gotten by us!' But it wasn't the *Rheem* at all, but a Richfield ship, the *Larry H. Doheny*, anchored alongside the Standard pier. We went alongside, and the crew told us they had been fired upon by a sub with a torpedo which exploded prematurely. Where it hit the water, I don't know, but its concussion broke the cabin doors on the wheelhouse. But no hit."

According to Merle, the *Doheny's* crew claimed that a pair of torpedoes was sent her way, both missing. Some believe that these may have come to shore, producing a "deep, powerful thud."

Molinari continued: "It was then about 7 or 8 o'clock, and after we talked a bit, we proceeded to dock, only to be met by our boss, William Shimeyer, who asked us to have a look up the coast where a ship was rumored to have been sunk, the *Montebello*. It was then that Nielsen came out to board the *Alma* for the rescue search. I can't recall the other crew members who joined us—maybe Glen Bickford or C.D. Sissel—who were on the launch *Estero*. And then somewhere between Point Estero and where the radar domes now are (editors' note: this site was just south of Cambria), we sighted two lifeboats from the *Montebello*. They were in fairly heavy seas, kind of close to shore and rowing down the coast. We picked up 22 people in two lifeboats in our boat, and Pete Stocking picked up ten in one lifeboat. We turned around and took them to Cayucos. No one was injured."

The remaining crew members of the *Montebello* put in near Cambria on a rocky promontory of the Sibley ranch.

Censorship at that point must have been embryonic (but blackouts already were a habit), as the accounts in the *Call-Bulletin* give the locale of the ship's grave as "four miles off the California coast." The *Telegram-Tribune*, however, gave the details as to the location.

A Japanese monograph (by way of the Chief of Military History, U.S. Army Department of Army) indicates that Nippon's plans were to follow the attack on Pearl Harbor with concerted attacks along our entire West Coast.

Jane Bailey, co-author of the definitive Morro Bay's Yesterdays, *wrote this story for Vol. 4, No. 2 of* La Vista.

WARTIME INTEREST

Soldiers will soon shave with plastic razors, thus helping to conserve metals, the War Department says. Cases likewise will be made of plastic materials, and both razor and case have been tested for ability to take severe variations in temperature and extraordinary abuse.

—*SHOT 'N SHELL*, June 10, 1942

Art Criddle

BREAKWATER WORKER TELLS HOW WAR HIT MORRO BAY

War activity really began to show in Morro Bay in late 1940. I went to work on the dredge which was really one of the first parts of the breakwater job in November of 1941. At that time we knew that something was stirring.

Of course, right after Pearl Harbor we had to dim all our lights. As a matter of fact we had to drive on the highway with just our car's parking lights on, and this was very useless as we had a lot of fog in those days. But there wasn't much traffic, so it really wasn't so bad. We were rationed to four and one-half gallons of gasoline a week so we didn't do much unnecessary driving.

The first real excitement happened in the December of 1941. One morning about 4 o'clock, we were practically shaken out of bed by a terrific explosion. We jumped up and ran outside. It happened that a Japanese submarine's torpedo had missed the *SS Heilman*, a tanker which was en route from El Segundo to Richmond, and had hit Morro Rock underwater.

When that tanker left El Segundo, the captain knew he was being followed by a submarine, so to elude it he put in at Avila harbor and laid over there until after dark. He then cautiously proceeded out and started north up the coast. But the submarine was waiting for him. And when the tanker was west of Morro Rock, the submarine fired at the tanker, missing it and hitting the rock.

After running outside in response to the blast, we stayed out in our yard for probably an hour. A few people had come by and stopped, and we were talking with them when suddenly we heard gun fire and could see flashes north and west of Cayucos. That was when that same submarine sank the *SS Montebello*. *(Editor's note: The Japanese submarine used its deck guns to fire on the sinking ship's crew as they went into the lifeboat.)*

We lived out on old Highway 1 about a mile and one-half north of Morro Bay. A battalion of soldiers was stationed at the then famous old hotel called the Cloisters Inn, which was on the beach and just a little north of our house. Of course, it's gone now.

Different units of the army used to march about every day all the way from San Luis Obispo out to that old hotel and back. I remember the little scouting planes that used to fly low and at terrific speeds right down the highway just above the heads of those soldiers as part of their training. The planes would go back and forth for what seemed like several hours.

There were many gun emplacements across from our house along the beach, down in the fields and along the Estero Bay beach as part of the preparations in case of an invasion.

About that time in early 1942 I found a boot on the beach. It was the kind of boot worn on submarines; its sole was wooden and there were no nails in it. The boot was brand new. Presumably, it was lost by a Japanese who had landed in a small boat on the beach. I believe this was the case because real early one morning the cavalry chased someone through our yard. We then heard that some Japanese had come ashore and been spotted but had escaped. I found the boot the next day. I turned in the boot at the office where I was working at the rock.

One of the little incidents that I have never read about was that right after the torpedo exploded at Morro Rock there was a great exodus of people from Morro Bay, going over the Atascadero road that day. I don't know where they went or how long they stayed, but we apparently really had a land rush going over there.

Of course, there were many rumors during the war, and very few could be verified. One rumor which was very persistent was that a little, two-man Japanese submarine had come ashore at Pismo Beach. I don't believe I ever talked with anyone who actually saw it, but we kept hearing the story.

When the breakwater project was started, it was said to be a future submarine base. After progressing for a year or so, they changed the designation to a landing barge station. Later it became a harbor project.

WARTIME HUMOR

Jeeps Glorified by Tin Pan Alley

Our Jeeps, bless 'em, are getting richly deserved praise—in song.

A compilation of songs on the market with the little rascals as a theme, shows six melodic tributes.

These late releases of Tin-Pan Alley bear the titles—"Keep the Jeep Ajumpin'," "Johnny Got a Jeep," "Little Bo Peep Has Lost Her Jeep," "The Jeep Song," "The Jeeps Are Coming," and "Six Jerks and a Jeep."

—SHOT 'N SHELL, May 20, 1942

Famous last words:

AT THE PAY TABLE: But, Sir, they always let me have seconds in the mess hall.

—SHOT 'N SHELL, April 1, 1942

Dan Krieger

CIVILIAN HEROICS SAVED OIL TANKER'S CREWMEN

Despite the construction of three large military facilities at Camp San Luis, Camp Roberts and Camp Cooke, the Central Coast was not prepared for the events of Christmastide 1941.

The *Telegram-Tribune's* headlines for December 23 read: "Jap Sub Sinks Tanker Here—36 Crewmen Saved In Three Lifeboats." The 8,000-ton Union Oil tanker *Montebello* had been hit in her empty center-hold by a torpedo from a large Japanese submarine off the coast of Cambria. The tanker sank in about 20 minutes. The submarine surfaced, and members of her crew sprayed small arms fire on the *Montebello's* three lifeboats as they retreated toward shore.

The entire crew was saved. "A Christmas miracle," in the words of many local residents. A great part of that miracle can be attributed to the heroism of residents of Cambria, Cayucos and Morro Bay—all of them civilians who risked their lives in the rescue effort.

Among the rescuers was Austin Waltz, editor of *The Cambrian*. Waltz also was a "stringer" for the *San Francisco Call-Bulletin*, the only major newspaper to feature the story.

Secretary of the Navy Frank Knox and Lieutenant General John L. DeWitt, commander of the Western Defense Command, were unable to prevent the publication of the *Call-Bulletin's* article, although the censors eliminated many specific details. Later, the "official position" of the Navy was that the submarine raid never happened.

Waltz was joined in the rescue effort by J. Neil Moses, who served both as a reporter for *The Cambrian* and as editor of the *Morro Bay Sun*, which was printed at *The Cambrian's* plant and which used that paper's mailing permit.

Moses, who died in 1977, wrote this dramatic account of the rescue for *The Cambrian's* January 1, 1942, issue:

"Four men were seen straining at the oars. Another was bailing water. A sixth man, obviously the skipper of the torpedoed tanker *Montebello*, was sitting tensely at the stern of the lifeboat, using an oar for a tiller.

"The sea was a tempest, and the wind was blowing a gale. On they came, slowly, laboriously. They were heading for the rocks, but they couldn't help it. With each mountainous swell it looked like the storm-tossed lifeboat would capsize. They were taking the sea broadsides all the way. Maybe it was because they were green hands at the oars; possibly because they didn't have the strength to right the boat against the wind and current.

"On they came, inching closer and closer to exposed and partially submerged rocks. They were straining with every ounce of energy they

This life jacket from the *Montebello* is held by George Sheffield. *Photo courtesy of the* Morro Bay Sun-Bulletin.

possessed, but it looked like they were doomed to crack up on a jagged 20 feet of the outcropping. The skipper, for reasons unexplained, plunged into the sea and made it to the rock just as a big swell struck him. He was unable to grasp anything and the back-sweep of the swell carried him 30 yards out.

"Finally the lifeboat crashed into the shore rock. It was hard to re-count what happened after that. There was a wild scramble by four of the men. One or two of them made it after a drenching. Two others floundered in the sea but managed to hang on to the lines.

"A husky young man, who turned out to be David Chase of Morro Bay, had stripped and plunged into the sea to take a line to the skipper who was held afloat by his lifebelt. The skipper was too exhausted to struggle and was just drifting in the swells. By using an oar, Chase finally made contact and the two were towed in.

"In another corner, Jack Freebody, Cambria fire chief, was struggling to help one of the victims out of the boiling sea and was swept off the rock and considerably bashed up before the two were hauled in.

"The last to be rescued was a small man with little meat on his bones. He clung desperately to a line and twice was able to mount a low rock ledge only to be swept off by successive swells. Again he clambered onto the ledge, and this time I managed to get down in time to help him to his feet. I secured the line around his waist, hitched up his drooping dungarees that were hindering his movement and gave him a boost up over the rock and to safety. A couple of swells took my measure. (But there were no heroics. I only got a drenching, which was enough to make me a confirmed land-lubber.)

"In the meantime, the sixth man, Fireman Edgar F. Smith, perhaps the wisest of the lot, had stayed with the boat. It drifted around the outjutting rock and into a very small cove. A swell lifted its bow momen-tarily onto a rock and Smith climbed on it and there remained out of reach of the water until he had rested. When he later climbed the bluff, he came up vigorously swearing at the Japs.

"The little fellow I gave a hand to suffered the worst of the lot. He was a pitiable sight, spotted with oil, gaunt, blue and pallid white. Some minutes later when he was lying on the ground rolled in blankets, I asked him his name. He tried hard to tell me but I couldn't make it out. His teeth were chattering up. They had to carry him up to the road where he was placed in a truck.

"John T. Smith of Torrance, Bill Frez of Westville, Massachusetts, and Captain Olaf Eckstrom were the only other names of survivors I could get.

"And that's the rescue as I saw it. Each one in the party tried to do his bit. Dave Chase did the heroics. He risked his life to get to Capt. Olaf

Sailor beware!

LOOSE TALK } CAN COST LIVES }

Eckstrom. Chief Freebody was in there punching every minute and was in a bad way for a moment. The rest of us did our stuff from comparative safety.

"The irony of it all came when I was driving back to the printing office. Two young Japanese-American soldiers were driving the Army ambulances going up to pick up the survivors."

This article first appeared in the San Luis Obispo County Telegram-Tribune.

Part 6

ODYSSEY

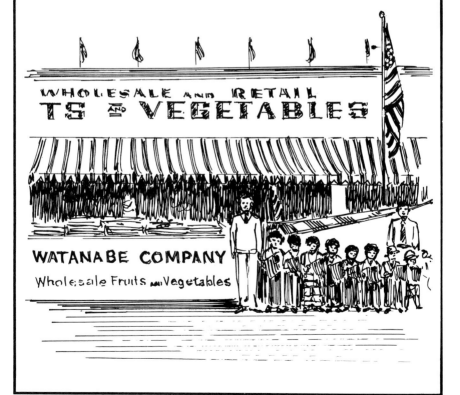

Dan and Liz Krieger

JAPANESE ODYSSEY IN THE MIDDLE KINGDOM

Visitors to San Luis Obispo on festive occasions like the Fourth of July or La Fiesta de las Flores during the late 1920s and 1930s observed the degree to which the Japanese residents had entered into the spirit of these "American" celebrations.

Entering town from the south on lower Higuera Street, the visitor would have passed by the Watanabe Co., a wholesale fruit and vegetable store located at the intersection of South Street. On July 4th of 1928, the Watanabe store was decked out with numerous American flags and patriotic bunting. Small flags surrounded the roof of the store and a large flag stood next to the gasoline pump as the Watanabe family and their friends posed for snapshots.

Later in the 1930s, observers noted a float bedecked with flowers and a Japanese motif sporting a large American flag for La Fiesta de las Flores, a traditional *Californio* festival created by an Irish Catholic priest, Father Daniel Keenan, to support the renovation of the old Mission San Luis Obispo de Tolosa. Still later, visitors saw a float encircled with an American flag and a banner reading "Japanese—Pismo Beach." And this float would win first prize in the Pismo Beach Pioneer Day Celebration on August 1, 1936.

Such historical vignettes of America's melting pot can be deceptive. Japanese had arrived in this county by 1904, and by the late 1920s, most of them had decided that America was their permanent home. But their road towards establishing new roots in this land was not an easy one.

The Japanese settlement in San Luis Obispo County conforms to the pattern of immigration that occurred in other agricultural regions of the Pacific Coast after 1869. Young men came here from Japan, working along the Southern Pacific Railroad route as farm laborers. Many of them saved enough money to lease land on which they could farm. The "Yellow Peril" propaganda had resulted in the Alien Land Laws of 1920 and 1921. Persons

Opposite page. Top: A Japanese Fourth of July float goes down Higuera Street in San Luis Obispo during the 1930s. *Photo courtesy of the Cal Poly Archives.* Middle: Japanese-American children holding American flags line the front of the Watanabe store on the corner of Higuera and South Streets on July 4, 1928. *Photo courtesy of Paul Kurokawa.* Bottom:This patriotic Japanese-American float won first prize in the 1936 Pioneer Day Celebration in Pismo Beach. *Photo courtesy of Lillian Sakurai.*

The Siichrido Shinoda family and two workers in an apricot orchard on the leased Thomas Hodges Ranch on Halcyon Road in Arroyo Grande, 1908. *Photo courtesy of Bennett-Loomis archives.*

born in Asia could not become citizens and were prohibited from owning title to land. Hence, there were very few family-owned farms at first. Eventually, the young men saved enough money to settle down and get married. Then they might have American-born children who could hold title to land.

The Japanese men usually married "picture brides" arranged by their families in Japan. They also would bring their brothers and friends here, organizing agricultural cooperatives to accommodate the newly-arrived young men. And while the Asian-born *Issei* could not become citizens, the children who were born in America and referred to as *Nisei* were automatically citizens. As citizens, they could own land in California. By 1941, two-thirds of the Japanese residents in San Luis Obispo County were American-born. This meant that more and more Japanese families were owning their own farms—very often in the names of their *Nisei* children.

Some of the very first Japanese who came to work in the Arroyo Grande Valley were confronted by hostile groups shortly after their arrival. The *Arroyo Grande Herald* for January 18, 1902, printed this report:

"In the dead stillness of night eight or ten Portuguese and Mexicans, so the story goes, went to the seed farm (Sperry Ranch in upper Arroyo Grande Valley) in disguise and broke into the house occupied by the Japanese laborers, rounded them up and…(took) them about two miles from the ranch, relieved them of a watch and other valuables and gave them two days to leave that locality….

"The Japs didn't go. On the contrary they came into town and bought guns galore and swore out complaints against several whom they recognized. Yesterday one J.C. Silva was arrested by Constable Bennett on complaint of S.

Shieaki and charged with house-breaking and burglary and brought before Justice Lowe. He pleaded not guilty and demanded $2 per day for every day that he lost on account of the charge. The Judge committed him to the keeping of the sheriff until examination. Other arrests will follow."

On January 25, 1902, the *Herald* reported that a man named Llewelling had been questioned about the incident, but had succeeded "in partially proving an alibi by showing that he was sick in bed up to 8 p.m. on the evening of the trouble." But the article went on to note that the "affair had developed a more serious phase...Instead of intimidation it is robbery as well. It is said that more arrests will follow."

The violence apparently had not subsided by March 22, 1902, when the *Herald* printed the following story under the headline "Getting Ready for an Attack:"

"A few days ago a young Japanese was brought into Dr. Clark's office with a bullet in his jaw...No amount of coaxing would reveal how it happened but careful hunting shows some curious facts: It develops that since the Japs had a visit from masked individuals a couple of months ago who wanted to scare them away from their job (sic) they have armed themselves with pistols and have regular target practice every Sunday. They are all more or less expert bicycle riders and they have set up the stuffed figure of a man a few yards from the road, and when the practice begins they mount their wheels and...dash by the dummy and fire a regular broadside at it. The chances are that the next band of maskers that visit the seed farm will meet with a very warm reception."

The article evidently intimidated future nighttime harassment of the Japanese workers in Arroyo Grande.

By the 1930s, the Japanese had become an integral part of the community in Arroyo Grande. Gordon Bennett, son of a pioneer Arroyo Grande family, recalls these experiences with the Japanese community as he was growing up:

"In our grammar school years there were many Japanese students in the Arroyo Grande Valley. John Loomis and I had many Japanese friends as classmates. In the late 1930s, the Loomis family put on an annual Japanese Picnic, usually at the Routhzan Park in upper Arroyo Grande Valley. This was always an exciting event since, besides the big barbecue, there were unlimited supplies of soda pop and ice cream. Japanese farmers and their families came from all over the county to attend the annual event."

Clearly, the Japanese families were entering the mainstream of life in the valley. On the eve of the Second World War, the Japanese were farming throughout the Central Coast, particularly in the Santa Maria, Arroyo Grande and Los Osos Valleys, as well as along the coastal plain stretching between Morro Bay and Cayucos. The area surrounding the Watanabe store on South Higuera Street in San Luis Obispo became the focal point for Japanese commercial activity. The complex included a grocery, a two-story hotel, a boarding house, a barber shop and an ice cream parlor.

The "center" was located directly across Higuera Street from the narrow gauge (Pacific Coast) railroad depot that had served the agricultural economy of the Central Coast since the late 1870's. It also was along the main trucking route, Highway 101. In fact, this was an excellent location for trans-coastal shipment and for recruiting seasonal labor.

From this point, along with locations in Pismo Beach, Oceano and Morro Bay, agricultural produce ranging from flower seed to winter peas, bush beans, pole beans and celery might be gathered together for shipment to San Francisco and Los Angeles and for transshipment elsewhere. Because of the value of these labor-intensive products, Japanese agriculture prospered—by relative standards even throughout the depression of the 1930s.

The 1930s were a point of coalescence for the Japanese community in San Luis Obispo County, as pioneer farmer Tameji Eto worked to organize the Southern Central Japanese Agricultural Association to protect the price of produce. Japanese language schools for educating the *Nisei* in their ancestral language and culture were promoted by the *Nihonjin-kai*, or Japanese Association, in four locations: on Cherry Street in Arroyo Grande, on the Eto property in the Los Osos Valley, in Pismo Beach, and near the original site of the Buddhist Temple on French Road adjacent to the present Madonna Inn property.

Mitsu and Yotsu Sakamoto recalled how they went to the Japanese school in Pismo Beach each school day after their regular classes. In 1941-42, Mitsu was in the ninth grade at Arroyo Grande High School, and Yotsu was in the eighth grade in Pismo Beach. Yotsu said she "wasn't really too thrilled about going" to the additional hours of schooling. Some Japanese families did not send their youngsters to the Japanese after-school program.

Students at the Japanese schools would attend five days a week after their regular public school activities. These schools were not restricted to the *Nisei*; Josephine Garcia Avila's parents wanted her to go to the school held at the Buddhist Temple on French Road because they had many Japanese tenants on their ranch, so Jo and her cousin, Dr. Luis Pereira, attended the school together. Jo recalls that her family received many wonderful presents from their Japanese tenants over the years, and Jo went on to study the Japanese language at the College of the Holy Names in Oakland, California.

While the Garcia-Pereira example of integration between the Japanese and non-Japanese communities is admittedly exceptional, Japanese adoption of American institutions was not. Baseball and Boy Scouts are examples

The Tameji Eto family in 1919. Eto, a pioneer Los Osos Valley farmer, was instrumental in organizing the Southern Central Japanese Agricultural Association to protect the price of produce. *Photo courtesy of Masaji Eto.*

of this adaptation. The Buddhist Temple sponsored Boy Scout troops, just as did the Christian churches.

There were both Buddhist and Christian families among the Japanese settlers. A Japanese Christian Church was founded in Santa Maria in 1929 and attended by the Kobara family in Arroyo Grande. The Ikeda family attended the Methodist Church in Arroyo Grande. Because so many of the Japanese settlers came from the areas around Hiroshima, Wakayama and Kumamoto, where Buddhism is very popular, perhaps as many as 90 per cent of the *Issei* population were Buddhist, but many of the *Nisei* who could speak English were Christian. Both faiths used the *Nihonjin* Hall in Arroyo Grande and shared the expense of establishing a Japanese language school.

The First Buddhist Church in Guadalupe had founded a Japanese Children's Home there in 1919 in response to unmet needs among the newly immigrated Japanese families. Students from as far away as Morro Bay and Lompoc would spend the school year there, attending Guadalupe's public schools during the day and studying the Japanese language and culture in the evening.

Paul Kurokawa, who was born in San Luis Obispo in 1915 and whose parents had a fruit and vegetable store, attended the children's home through the sixth grade. He entered the seventh grade at Court School in San Luis Obispo and was among the first *Nisei* to attend San Luis Obispo Junior High School. He became a student leader and athlete at San Luis Obispo High School. For financial reasons, he had to abandon his dream of attending the University of California and instead attended a university in Tokyo.

One of his best periods at the children's home was when one of his classmates contracted scarlet fever and the facility was placed under quarantine at Christmas time. "With due respect and apologies to Aki (the sick classmate), I confess that not being able to leave the building and go home for the holiday break was a pleasant bonus for me," he said. "Parents and friends were not allowed to enter the premises, but they brought many toys and gifts to the door. My parents, though very caring, were generally busy working throughout the holiday season."

Yotsu Sakamoto, who lived with her family in Pismo Beach next to her father's small grocery store on Cypress Avenue, said, "There wasn't a Buddhist Church in Pismo then, and my mother just wanted us to go to church, any church, just so we would get some religious training." Her

Opposite page. Top: The Japanese School of San Luis Obispo in 1928. *Photo courtesy of Paul Kurokawa.* Middle: Delegates of the San Luis Obispo Young Men and Women's Buddhist Association. *Photo courtesy of "Lefty" Nishijima.* Bottom: The Buddhist Temple-sponsored Boy Scouts of America troop in 1932. *Photo courtesy of Paul Kurokawa.*

sister, Mitsu, said they sometimes went to the Pismo Beach Presbyterian Church "but we weren't too religious about it." She added, "We liked the stickers and little things we kids got at church."

Relations with members of the non-Japanese community varied according to family. In Pismo Beach, Irene Carpenter reportedly would buy out Hills Bazaar late every autumn as she prepared gifts for the Japanese children of her area. According to a long-time resident, it is no exaggeration to say that she "introduced Christmas to most of the Japanese children of the South County in the 1920s."

Yotsu Sakamoto said, "At Christmas time, Irene Carpenter used to bring a cake with colorful sprinkles on it. She was a nice old lady. She'd come in an old Cadillac that my father later bought from her. Then we'd go driving in it on Sundays. He would use his other car, a LaSalle or Buick, taking out the back seat to transport vegetables that he bought for the store because he never had a pickup truck."

In the Los Osos Valley, Tameji Eto had excellent relations with his neighbors, the Turris, Mellos and Gianolinis. Masaji Eto recalls riding on the school bus with the children from these neighboring families and forming life-long friendships. Eto also points out how his father shared heavy farm equipment with Joe Turri, whose ranch was immediately to the south of the Eto farm.

The retail merchants in San Luis Obispo were generally friendly to the Japanese settlers. The Japanese maintained accounts at the Andre, Sauer and Muzio stores. Grocer J.J. Andre often said, "Don't worry. If you can't pay now, wait until the crops come in." These grocery stores, and the community in general, reciprocated in this commercial activity, buying fresh vegetables from peddlers driving produce trucks from the Watanabe, T. H. Kurokawa and Tanaka enterprises.

The Japanese were not passive members of the economic community. After Tameji Eto established his farm in the then-distant precincts of the Los Osos Valley in 1919, he had difficulty in maintaining communications with his business connections in Pismo Beach. He felt the need for a telephone link. Unfortunately, the telephone company in San Luis Obispo felt that it could not justify a long line to serve relatively few customers. So Eto joined with other valley residents in organizing the Los Osos Mutual Telephone Company with a subscription of 800 shares at $100 each. Later this company was bought out by the Bell System.

The Japanese community also contributed to the beautification of public buildings in a way that was both significant and appropriate. In 1931, just when Japan's troubles with the League of Nations were beginning over its invasion of Manchuria, the Japanese Association gave a gift of 100

Paul Kurokawa is second from left in the top row in this circa 1924 photo from Guadalupe Elementary School. *Photo courtesy of Paul Kurokawa.*

Suiko Hori, Hatsumi Tashiro and Reiko Hori in front of the Pismo Beach Japanese school's teacher's home. *Photo courtesy of "Lefty" Nishijima.*

cherry trees to the new San Luis Obispo High School campus. Cherry trees were planted along the driveway leading to the main building and in a grove near the home economics building. Removal of some of these trees began in the late 1950's, and the last were removed in 1978 because of disease. But for more than two decades, they made San Luis High School a place of spectacular beauty.

Of course, the cherry trees were a symbol of Japanese culture and ties with the home island. These "ties" were going to provide justification for the unprecedented action of the United States government in removing the Japanese—the majority of whom were *Nisei*—a decade later. Because of this unfortunate circumstance of wartime panic, the nature of the relationship between the peoples of Japanese ancestry in our country and the Japanese homeland is worthy of comment.

First, it is necessary to note that from the 1880s until 1952, immigrants from Asia were automatically denied the right to become American citizens. The children of the *Issei*, known as *Nisei*, were American citizens, of course, by virtue of being born on American soil. Nonetheless, under the rules of a practice adhered to by the nations of Italy, Switzerland and Germany—at least until 1919—persons of parentage from those and many other lands were, by virtue of "right of blood" (*jus sanquinis*), always claimed as citizens of the parents' (usually the father's) native land.

Hence, dual citizenship was commonly held by many *Nisei*. That is, if your parents were born in Japan, you were a citizen of both Japan and the United States.

All of this changed in 1925. The Japanese Exclusion Act of 1925 prompted the Japanese government to revise its policies. Any person of Japanese descent born abroad after December 1, 1925, was automatically released from the claim of Japanese citizenship unless the parents registered the child within 14 days of birth with the Japanese Consul. Hence, thousands of *Nisei* born after 1925 were purely American citizens.

While many *Issei* residents of the county registered their children largely out of fear that they one day might be excluded from these shores, others did not. The Japanese-American Citizen's League urged *Issei* parents not to register their children, insuring the purely American character of the *Nisei*.

On December 31, 1941, the *San Luis Obispo County Telegram-Tribune* (the *T-T*) reported that the census had revealed 925 persons of Japanese ancestry in this county (out of a total population of 48,000 as of January of 1942 as estimated by the California Taxpayers Association). Of the Japanese, 639, or more than two-thirds of the total, were citizens of the United States. Yet county newspapers had little to say regarding the worsening Japanese-American relations until October of 1941.

On October 15, 1941, the *T-T* observed that "many people of Japanese, German and Italian origins, for instance, are dual citizens of this country and of their homeland." The paper favored legislation proposed by Secretary of War Henry Stimson that would force individuals to choose between American citizenship and the nationality of their parents.

Coincidentally, in that same issue, the newspaper headlined "Japanese Intensify Attack on the United States." The article focused on the worsening relations between the two nations while noting that among the many American citizens repatriated to the United States during this time were some 300 *Nisei.*

The next day, the *T-T* observed further difficulties on the international scene as the pro-peace government of Prince Konoye was ousted by the more bellicose Hideki Tojo in Tokyo.

Ironically, the first *T-T* editorial comment on the serious nature of Japanese-American relations occurred just the day before Pearl Harbor. There were numerous anti-Nazi editorials, but none dealing with the deteriorating conditions in East Asia.

On Saturday, December 6, 1941, the *T-T's* "Sam Luis" remarked, "To Japan: You can't carry water on both shoulders like that. You are likely to get your feet wet." The editorial was referring to Japan's attempting to deal with both China and America at the same time. By this point, the fleet of Admiral Yamamoto was less than 500 miles from Pearl Harbor.

There was another irony during that first week of December of 1941. Paul Kurokawa, a native of San Luis Obispo and a graduate of Meiji University in Tokyo, spoke to a political science class at San Luis Obispo Junior College that week and assured the students that a transpacific war, given the great distances involved, was unlikely. Among the factors that led him to this conclusion was his involvement in international trade which included having an American football team visit Japan as part of an effort to promote American-Japanese friendship.

The following Sunday, he and his wife, Betty, were in a motion picture theater in Santa Maria when the assault on Pearl Harbor was announced.

The outbreak of hostilities drastically altered the circumstances of San Luis Obispo County's Japanese-American residents. The county had been on a war footing since late 1940 with the construction of major military installations at Camp Roberts and Camp San Luis Obispo. However grim the situation might have seemed vis-a-vis Japan, the mood on the homefront was one of people pulling together. On July 7, 1941, the *T-T* had editorialized that "America Needs ALL Her Strength" in a plea that said:

"We are a people made up of many peoples. In that lies strength, not weakness... We glory in our differences, and we feel that in them is

A Japanese-American soldier participates in the 1941 Obon Festival at the Buddhist Temple in San Luis Obispo. *Photo courtesy of "Lefty" Nishijima.*

strength, for each group has something definite to contribute...The thing that binds us all together in the United States is not a phony racial doctrine, but the joyous and spontaneous loyalty of diverse peoples who have learned to live together, and found it good....

"The test is not 'Who are you?' but 'What can you do?' It is wise and right that both in the military services and in defense industries, broadening opportunities should be gradually opening up (and they are) to Americans of colored blood. It is wise and right that America should not deprive itself (as Germany has done) of the loyal service of Jews and Catholics because of their race or religion. It is wise and right that America, fostering mother of a hundred races, religions and peoples, should call on all alike to defend her. That is our strength. Let us use it."

The Japanese were called upon to serve in the military and other areas of U.S. national defense. Many *Nisei* boys in the county had been classified in the early rounds of Selective Service activity. On January 6, 1941, the *T-T* reported that Toshio Nakamura, Yonehisa Yamagami, Munetoshi G. Horiuchi, Hiroshi Nakamura, Takashi Yukitake and Jack Fukushima had received their notices of classification.

Under a heading of "5 Japanese Selectees Feted Here" on February 19, 1941, the paper observed:

"Hailing their coming year's training as a 'first chance to show loyalty and obedience to the land of their birth,' five county boys of Japanese descent...at the Anderson Hotel were given a 'send off' by nearly 150 county members of the San Luis Obispo Japanese-American League and the

San Luis Obispo Japanese Association.

"The honored draftees were Jack Fukushima of San Luis Obispo, Sadami Fujita of Arroyo Grande called by the San Luis Obispo Board, Jimmie Kawamura and Teroaka Sakai of Cambria, and William Nagano of Morro Bay, called by the Paso Robles Board.

"'It makes us feel good to know we have your support,' Nagano stated to the members of the Japanese organization. 'We know that our conduct in service will reflect on all Japanese-Americans in the United States and we will do our very best.'"

San Luis Obispo Mayor Fred Kimball was quoted several paragraphs later as saying: "The importance of your training to all of us is that the upbuilding of our army has a tendency to bring us all together, shoulder to shoulder for the protection of our democracy."

A much larger party for Japanese-American soldiers was held later. On October 25, 1941, the *T-T* bore this two column headline on page one: "Japanese-American Group To Fete Soldiers Sunday." The article announced that the Japanese-American Citizens League in San Luis Obispo was planning a dinner and dance to be held at the San Luis Obispo Senior High School to honor Japanese soldiers of American descent (that's how the newspaper phrased it) at Camp San Luis Obispo and Camp Roberts. Expected to attend were 500 visitors, including leaders of the Japanese community from the Los Angeles area.

On the following Monday, the *T-T* reported that the dinner dance had been attended by more than 1,000 persons. Major Samuel Pickett, representing Camp San Luis Obispo Commandant Colonel Henry Bull, spoke about the important work which Japanese-American soldiers were doing for national defense. Some 150 leaders of the Japanese community in Los Angeles had come for the event. The Cal Poly Orchestra played, and Karl Taku, president of the San Luis Obispo Chapter of the Japanese-American Citizens League, chaired the program. Mary Eto acted as hostess and introduced Mayor Kimball, who welcomed the out-of-town dignitaries. C.L. Smith, school board secretary, and Sheriff Murray Hathaway also were in attendance, as was Captain Earl Hunting, the officer in charge of morale at Camp San Luis Obispo.

From this attendance, we can presume that the San Luis Obispo community as a whole recognized the importance of the Japanese community as America prepared for war.

The Japanese communities donated plants and trees to Camp San Luis. On October 13, 1941, the *T-T* reported that at the behest of a Japanese-American, Private First Class George Muto, a soldier in Company K, 159th Infantry, nearly 10,000 trees and shrubs had been donated to Camp

San Luis. They arrived in 20 Army trucks and were accepted by Major J.M. Walker of the Military Police, who was in charge of camp beautification. Major Walker had traveled to Los Angeles with 45 soldiers to pick up the plants and trees. There the group attended a luncheon given by the Central Japanese Association of America and the Japanese Chamber of Commerce.

Thus the Japanese-American community was very much a part of the war effort in this county when disaster struck. Perhaps this fact—well known to many county residents—moderated the impact of Pearl Harbor and prevented much of the initial hysteria against Japanese residents that occurred in other areas of the Pacific Coast.

The reaction of the *T-T* to the news of Pearl Harbor in terms of the nearly 1,000 Japanese residents in the county was extremely circumspect. On December 8, 1941, after spending much of the issue reporting what was known of the previous day's tragedy at Oahu, the newspaper was relatively restrained in its main editorial. Under the euphemism "One For All And All For One," it began patriotically: "Now let's get the Japanese!" But, by this, the editor clearly meant the Japanese Empire, for he went on to comment:

"San Luis Obispo County and the Pacific Coast generally is especially closely involved in the struggle. On the coast are the possible points of invasion and the concentration of most of the 150,000 Japanese who reside in the United States (sic).

"In considering the Japanese-Americans it must be kept in mind that while a few might still be loyal to the Land of the Rising Sun and plotting sabotage and treachery against the enemy of the emperor, most of the Japanese-Americans are loyal to the Stars and Stripes. Many are already in military service and making splendid records as soldiers.

"Interviewed by the *Telegram-Tribune*, the head of the local Japanese-American League today expressed the loyalty of the group to America. That is as it should be."

On page five of the same issue was this headline: "Japanese-American League Declares Loyalty To United States."

On December 9, the paper headlined "County Defense Unit Urges Civilian Calm." And on December 20 there was a reminder of "One For All And All For One" as the *T-T* reported "Camp Roberts Japanese Aid In New Defense." The article told about seven *Nisei* privates who, immediately following Pearl Harbor, had volunteered to teach Japanese language and customs to the officers of the 87th Infantry Training Battalion. Forty-seven officers signed up for the classes which were held twice a week.

While the *T-T* and community leaders generally were urging citizens to keep calm following Pearl Harbor, the inexorable forces of two great nations at war were certain to disrupt the harmonious relations that had existed between families of Japanese descent and their neighbors.

On December 8, 1941, President Franklin D. Roosevelt made his "Day of Infamy" speech and asked Congress for a Declaration of War against Japan. Secretary of the Navy Frank Knox made a hurried trip to the Hawaiian Islands to inspect the damage to the Pacific Fleet. On his return to Washington, he told reporters, "The most effective fifth column work of the entire war was done in Hawaii, with the possible exception of Norway." It was later proven that no fifth column activity existed in Hawaii, but the seeds of distrust had been sown and sprouted.

Already, United States government policies were creating difficulties for Japanese-Americans. On December 8, a wartime emergency measure froze all Japanese bank accounts. On December 11, the *T-T* reported "Jap (sic) Funds Freezing Hurts Here." With their bank accounts seized by a Federal receiver, the Japanese farmers could not pay their workers. Only those who had previously transferred their deposits to their *Nisei* children had negotiable assets. This caused a great deal of discontent as workers on Japanese-owned farms in Oso Flaco, Arroyo Grande and Cambria had to go without pay.

The situation was exacerbated by the fact that many of these wage laborers were Filipino. Manila, the capital of the Philippines, was under aerial bombardment, and a Japanese invasion of the islands seemed imminent.

Not all of the farm worker payrolls were strapped by the freeze on alien bank accounts. Ownership of the Nagano farm in Morro Bay had been transferred to William and Patrick Nagano. Since they were American-born, their assets were not subject to any restrictions. All of their Filipino workers received full pay.

The hostility which this situation produced was tragically illustrated several weeks later when a small headline in the *T-T* noted "Japanese Formerly at S.L.O. Camp Stabbed to Death." Larry K. Tasaka, a 31-year-old *Nisei*, had been found stabbed to death on a Los Angeles street. In his pocket was found a certificate indicating that he had been given an honorable discharge from the Army Medical Corps' 26th Station Hospital Corps at Camp San Luis Obispo and referring to his character as "excellent." A Filipino had been arrested for his murder.

Mitsu Sakamoto said, "We were taunted on the school buses after Pearl Harbor, but what could we do but ignore it. We were outnumbered. One kid, when taunted, used to say, 'I may be yellow on the outside, but I'm white on the inside'."

However, Lillian Nishijima Sakurai, who was born in the family's home near Pirate's Cove, recalled a different experience. Remembering that she was a ninth grader at Arroyo Grande High School at the time, she said,

Left: Mr. and Mrs. Tsutsumi and daughter, Yoshiko, owned property at the corner of Eto (now Brook Street) and South Higuera Streets. Right: Mr. Watanabe and his daughter. Watanabe owned a fruit and vegetable store in San Luis Obispo and was known for constructing patriotic parade floats. *Photos courtesy of Paul Kurokawa.*

"I never felt any prejudice in the county after Pearl Harbor. But when we moved to Delano, I found that the Japanese, Mexicans and 'black' Russians (or Eurasians) lived on the 'wrong side of the track' and went to a separate high school."

The same newspaper article which reported the freezing of Japanese bank accounts indicated a continued sensitivity to the awkward position in which loyal Japanese-Americans found themselves. There also was a large measure of concern for the welfare of the economy of the county if agricultural workers could not be paid. The newspaper pointed out that some local Japanese who had their accounts frozen also had sons in the United States Army.

The payroll impasse was resolved in January of 1942, when the *T-T* announced "Order Will Permit Produce Operation By Japanese Here." The Treasury Department had devised a plan that would "liquidate money owed to San Luis Obispo County Filipinos by Japanese businessmen and…restore vegetable and produce production here to levels equal to those of last year." A special licensing order had been enacted whereby licensed Japanese nationals who had continuously resided in the United States since June of 1940 could pay wages in any amount to employees other than Japanese nationals. Pay to Japanese nationals was restricted to $100 per calendar month.

Meanwhile, fears of a Japanese naval attack on the Central Coast were increasing. On December 19, the *T-T* had its first really provocative headline: "Treachery And Violence Principal Weapons Of Japan's Fifth Column." What followed was a reprint of a United Press wire service story suggesting that members of that "fifth column...may be fishermen off lonely coasts reporting the habits of American air patrols...."

Charles Brown was General Foreman of the Pacific Coast Railway from World War I until just before Pearl Harbor. He recalled that Japanese commercial sailors on shore leave were taking photographs of virtually every site along the coast. Americans didn't have sufficient contact with mainland Japanese to understand that nation's love affair with the camera. Hence, a cultural expression was misinterpreted as probable espionage. Memories of camera-carrying Japanese contributed to popular hysteria after December 7th.

The United Press article might well have been regarded as simply another bit of wartime hysteria were it not for submarine attacks on United States shipping off the Central Coast commenced. The Standard Oil tanker *H.M. Storey* was attacked off Point Arguello, 40 miles south of San Luis Obispo. The *Storey* had been fired upon by the deck gun of a submarine which submerged after failing to damage the tanker. The *T-T* reported the following Monday that the unharmed tanker was sailing towards Estero Bay.

Other attacks were reported and corroborated off the West Coast near Monterey, Cape Mendocino and "between San Francisco and San Diego."

On Tuesday, December 23, the Union Oil tanker *Montebello* was sunk off Cambria by a "big submarine." Later that day, the *T-T*, just below its main editorial titled "The Larger Cause," quoted United States Attorney General Francis S. Biddle: "We will apprehend the alien troublemakers, but will protect the others against persecution and injustice." This statement was to have an ominous bearing on the future for San Luis Obispo County residents who happened to be of Japanese descent.

On December 30, the *T-T* reported in a small headline that "County Aliens Turn In Radios, Cameras, Guns." Non-citizen residents of Italian and German ancestry, as well as Japanese, were required to turn the restricted items over to county sheriff Murray Hathaway or to the chief of police in the city where they were living.

The article indicated that mainly cameras and radios were turned in, since, by law, aliens could not own firearms with the exception of "fowling pieces."

In the meantime, according to oral testimony of one observer: "Japanese stores were liquidating everything and trying to get the little they could out of it. They were selling fishing poles for $1.50 when a good split bamboo pole normally cost $25 and more."

The storekeepers' actions reflect the mood of concern in the county's Japanese community. The *Issei* and *Nisei* had become a significant element in the community. Their economic importance was most clearly recognized when payrolls were cut off following the freezing of alien checking accounts. The Japanese had participated in the American way of life from business activities to celebrating the Fourth of July and playing the game of baseball. They had made substantial contributions to the community as in the case of the cherry trees at San Luis Obispo High School. Yet, although some had lived in this county for more than 30 years, both *Issei* and *Nisei* recognized their peril. Wars often can divide even the closest of families, so the Japanese community knew that many county residents were understandably uncertain about the loyalty of the descendants of Nippon.

There is no indication that a great deal of anti-Japanese prejudice existed in this county. Patrick Nagano, a life-long county resident who served in the intelligence section of the United States Army during the war, recalls that there was "some element of racial discrimination, but that was general throughout California."

Certainly the Japanese community had good friends among prominent non-Japanese county residents. These friends would be of great help in ameliorating the difficulties of the troubled days to come, but they could not prevent the impending tragedy of the relocation order.

Immediately after Pearl Harbor, hundreds of *Issei* who were regarded as leaders within the Japanese community were arrested either by the Federal Bureau of Investigation directly, or by local law enforcement agencies operating with instructions from the F.B.I. and United States military authorities.

In San Luis Obispo County, the acknowledged leader of the Japanese community was Tamejii Eto of Los Osos, who was generally regarded as the first Japanese resident of the county. He was arrested on the evening of December 7, when Sheriff Murray C. Hathaway and a number of deputies went to the Eto ranch just off Los Osos Valley Road.

Tamejii Eto had been an upstanding member of the San Luis Obispo community, but also was a Japanese national of considerable importance. During the 1920s and 1930s, many delegations from Japan—especially those dealing with agricultural training—visited the Eto ranch. Unfortunately, these contacts, along with the leadership role played by the Eto family in the affairs of the Japanese community, caused the senior Eto to be singled out for arrest as a potential risk in times of national emergency.

Over the next three months, many *Issei* heads of families on the Central Coast were arrested. Most were abruptly turned over to the Federal Bureau of Investigation at Sharpes Park in coastal San Mateo County. They

The Hiyoshi Nishijima family. From left: Hiyoshi and his young daughter, Lillian; Lillian's uncle, "Lefty;" Haru with baby, Lloyd; Tsuyaru; and the Nishijima grandmother, Masa. *Photo courtesy of Lillian Nishijima Sakurai.*

The Nishijima children. From left: Paul, Tsuyara, Alice and Lillian. There were nine children in the Nishijima family born before the forced relocation in 1942. Lillian Nishijima Sakurai was the only child who would eventually be able to move back to San Luis Obispo County. *Photo courtesy of Lillian Nishijima Sakurai.*

were held *incommunicado* for several months until they were shipped to newly prepared prison camps in North Dakota. In many cases, their families didn't know what had happened to them for more than a year. Some weren't reunited with their families until the end of the war.

Not all who were arrested were prominent in the Japanese community, according to Mitsu and Yotsu Sakamoto. They said, "Our father was not a leader. He was nobody." Their father, Kaicha Sakamoto, was on the board of the Japanese school in Pismo Beach, but that was because he liked to attend the wrestling and boxing matches in an arena that was one block from his Pismo Beach store.

Mitsu explained the matter this way: "My father liked to spend all his free time at the matches, so the only way to get him to attend parents' meetings at the school was to elect him to the board." But Mr. Sakamoto was shipped off to North Dakota with the leaders of Japanese communities.

Mitsu Sakamoto recalls that "our father was sent to North Dakota shortly after Pearl Harbor, and we wouldn't see him for more than a year."

Masaji Eto recalls a prewar Superior Court Judge as saying, "We hardly ever have any trouble with the Japanese people." But that wasn't enough to procure the release of Masaji's father or even to obtain information about the place of his detention.

The Japanese community was quite naturally anxious to prove its loyalty. Included among the articles in the *T-T* on December 8 was one headlined "Japanese-American League Declares Loyalty To U.S." It said:

"We are American citizens—it (the attack on Pearl Harbor) doesn't affect us in any other way. (Karl Taku, president of the Japanese-American League) pointed to the large number of Japanese-American citizens in the United States Army as a definite indication of the sincerity of the citizens.

"He (Karl Taku) cited the peace time work and activities of the citizens and emphasized the excellent record of the Japanese residents and citizens of the United States in the light of law violations.

"'The number of Japanese juvenile delinquents and criminal offenders is very low,' he said."

Such statements, although true, were of no avail.

Some hostile feelings toward Japanese-Americans along the Pacific Coast had existed since the turn of the century. These sentiments were greatly intensified following the Japanese invasion of China in 1937.

Immediately after Pearl Harbor, a number of influential groups began to call for the removal of Japanese people, including *Nisei*, from coastal areas. These groups included the California Department of the American Legion and many local Posts; the California Farm Bureau; the Associated Farmers; the Grower-Shipper Vegetable Association and some labor unions.It seems obvious that many farmers wanted to acquire Japanese land!

Columnists, ranging from the highly respected Walter Lippmann to the sensationalist Westbrook Pegler, joined in the hue and cry for evacuating the Japanese.

On December 16, 1941, the *T-T* informed its readers that Japanese, Italian and German nationals over the age of 13 were instructed by the State Department to re-register with appropriate authorities by February 7, 1942. A month later, the newspaper was reporting that the San Luis Obispo Grange unanimously passed a resolution advocating the "movement of the Japanese from Pacific Coast areas...."

On January 24, 1942, the *T-T* printed an anonymous letter on its editorial page. That letter reflects the mounting mood of hysteria that existed along the West Coast in the days following Pearl Harbor and is charged with racist sentiments of the sort that wartime conditions produce. The letter began with a statement questioning the loyalty of county residents of Japanese heritage, saying:

"A number of these so-called Loyal Japs are my friends, as far as friendship goes nowadays, but I have this to say both for and against them. They have been, as far as I know, good American citizens and possibly still are, with one reservation. Everyone should know you can take the man out of the country, but you cannot take the country out of the man, and this is certainly true of our Japanese-Americans. I doubt if there is one Jap, who at some time or other has not sent money home to help build Jap ships and ammunition that they are now so generously giving us a bad time with."
The letter went on to assert that members of the Japanese community knew who the fifth columnists were among their ranks, but, because of national loyalty, would not reveal these names. The letter demanded that the really "loyal" Japanese come forward with the information and concluded: "Mr. American Jap sympathizer, think this over and remember Pearl Harbor. We don't want the same thing to happen at Avila Harbor or any other harbor or our city." The letter was signed "An American Defense Worker."

Professional historians reading this epistle from "An American Defense Worker" are struck by the highly literate vocabulary and syntax. Its economical use of words suggests journalistic skills. Could it be that the "American Defense Worker" was an employee of the newspaper, seeking to prepare the readers for a shift in editorial policy that was in line with national thinking?

That editorial shift took place five days later. On January 29, 1942, the newspaper, which heretofore had been generally sympathetic to the plight of the Japanese community, editorialized on "The Japanese Alien Menace."

The editorial was not aimed at persons of Japanese ancestry who, by virtue of American birth, were United States citizens, but that subtle distinction already had been lost in the panic that followed Pearl Harbor and the torpedoing of the *Montebello*. It began:

"What shall be done about the alien Japanese in San Luis Obispo County and other coastal regions where fifth columnists might strike telling blows at America's defense effort? Should they be sent inland, as advocated by the local American Legion Post, the state Legion and other organizations?"

The editorial went on to recount the experience of the British forces charged with the defense of Hong Kong, which had fallen victim to alleged fifth column activities. The editor added a note of restraint by asserting, "All Japanese cannot and should not be accused in one sweeping indictment."

The *T-T* editor pointed out that many county Japanese-Americans were in the armed services of the United States and that loyal Japanese-Americans had given many valuable tips to the F.B.I., leading to the arrest of "a good many spies and saboteurs...." The generosity of the Japanese to the Red Cross and other charitable organizations also was mentioned.

Nonetheless, the editor concluded:

"But no one wants to experience a West Coast Pearl Harbor, then say afterward what 'we should have done.' The time to remove the menace, and send the Japanese back to less vulnerable points inland, is before any such debacle can take place."

On February 3, 1942, a letter in the *T-T* addressed itself to the letter from "An American Defense Worker" and to a number of other unsigned letters referring to fifth column activities which had appeared in the newspaper since early January. In a signed letter, Ellsworth Petersen of San Luis Obispo observed:

"...Recently in the reader's column of your paper has been printed one of the longest series of un-American letters I have ever had the misfortune to read. I refer to those pseudopatriots who actually asked for the incarceration of American citizens who in turn have evidenced nothing but the sincerest loyalty."

Two days later, Daniel Kingsman applauded Ellsworth Petersen's comments, suggesting that the earlier letters had "almost all been cloaked in anonymity (which) made them even more questionable. Why in a free country are people afraid to be identified with their ideas? Or are they ashamed of them?" Kingsman went on to suggest that the anonymous authors of such letters were behaving like the very enemies America was at war with, asserting, "One doesn't 'defend America' by becoming a 'Nazi,' either in thought, word, or deed."

The letters of Petersen and Kingsman, as well as several anonymous letters sympathetic to the Japanese in the county, probably reflected the sentiments of many citizens of San Luis Obispo County, but they were running against the tide. West Coast officials, led by California State Attorney General Earl Warren, were actively in favor of evacuating persons of Japanese descent into the interior regions.

General John L. DeWitt, the commandant of the Western Defense Command area, did not wish to see the West Coast become the victim of a new Pearl Harbor surprise attack, and so the plans for a mass evacuation of the Japanese were begun. On Thursday, February 19, 1942, President Roosevelt signed Executive Order 9066, which granted the Army, through the Secretary of War, authority to define "military areas" from which "any and all persons may be excluded." The order also provided for "transportation, food, shelter, and other accommodations as may be necessary" for such persons "until other arrangements are made."

General DeWitt began a phased evacuation of the Japanese from coastal areas immediately. While the evacuation ultimately was to take eight months, the Japanese residents of San Luis Obispo County, because of their proximity to the coast, were effected immediately.

Helen Foree Keller, a teacher at Emerson School in San Luis Obispo, recalled the day before their evacuation. Helen had taught Japanese-American students when they were in first or second grade. In February of 1942, they were in the sixth grade. On rainy days over the past few years, Helen had driven her young friends to the Japanese Language School adjoining the Buddhist Temple on French Road at the end of the regular school day. Then, in one week in mid-February of 1942, 75 children, mainly *Nisei*, were dropped from the rolls of San Luis Obispo city schools as the evacuation reached its full momentum.

On their last day of school, Helen took the six students home for lunch. The following day they were gone. She continued to receive letters from three of the students who went to lunch with her that day: Lucy Tanaka, Florence Watanabe and Helen Kurozumi. In her home, Helen had some lovely Japanese porcelain, gifts from the Watanabe family before they left. Helen's close friend, Ella Fern Hall of San Luis Obispo, also had a Japanese teapot from someone among the evacuees she was kind to. Other families, too, received precious items from evacuees who were limited in how much they could take to the camps.

County opinion on the removal of the Japanese continued to be somewhat mixed. On January 30, 1942, the *T-T* headlined "Enemy Aliens To Be Moved From Coast Areas." The article dealt with United States Attorney General Francis Biddle's order that all German, Italian and Japanese aliens—meaning non-citizens, or *Issei* in the case of the Japanese—were to be removed from coastal areas by February 24. Coastal areas were defined as areas west of California Highway 1 in this county.

In that same issue of the newspaper there was another headline: "Chamber Requests Japanese Removal." The Board of Directors of the San Luis Obispo Chamber of Commerce had taken a vote and now urged the removal of the Japanese from the West Coast.

At the same time, key economic groups within the county saw difficulties resulting from the evacuation. On February 3, 1942, the *T-T* reported "Dairy, Produce Farmers See Labor Shortage With Relocation Of Enemy Aliens." The owners of some of the leading dairy and produce farms were concerned by the potential labor shortage which would occur following evacuation. Labor already was in short supply as a result of conscription and voluntary enlistments in the armed forces. These farmers "offered to bond their (alien) workers if such action is permitted, indicating that already serious labor shortages hampered normal production."

Despite fears of a labor shortage in county agriculture, military and law enforcement officials' concern over the Japanese presence predominated. The district attorney for San Luis Obispo County "advocated the placement of the Jap aliens in a concentration camp without any frills and just the bare necessities for life." He "...felt that the present restricted areas of the county were completely inadequate for efficient protection against sabotage."

Staff members of the War Relocation Authority in San Luis Obispo County later would refer to such xenophobic sentiments as "Nippomania."

The position of the Japanese community was most difficult at this time. With the attacks upon the oil tankers *Larry Doheny* and *Montebello* off the county's coast in late December of 1941, county residents were certain to be a bit paranoid. The shelling by a Japanese submarine of an oil refinery at Ellwood in Santa Barbara County (near the present University of California at Santa Barbara campus) on February 23, 1942, further reinforced such emotional fervor. At this moment of crisis, the Japanese-American Citizens League (JACL) emerged as a leadership force among the Japanese community.

The JACL was composed of young *Nisei* who, because of their American citizenship, felt that they could be more effective advocates for the Japanese community than their parents who were born in Japan. They were most frequently caught in the position of young leaders within a society that had traditionally been deferential to age.

When, in the first week of February of 1942, the registration of aliens over the age of 14 became law, the JACL attempted to ameliorate the situation. Anxious to reduce ill feelings among the non-Japanese community, Karl Taku, president of the county JACL, "offered its services in the regis-

General DeWitt, left, on a visit to Camp San Luis. DeWitt, military commander of the Pacific zone, urged adoption of Executive Order 9066. *Official photograph, Air Corps-U.S. Army, 91st Observation Squadron, Fort Lewis, Washington.*

tration just as the JACL (initials used in the *T-T* article) sided last month in the roundup of alien-owned radios, guns and other materials." Clearly, the JACL members were out to prove their unquestionable loyalty to America. But that was not going to be sufficient.

San Luis Obispo City Postmaster William C. O'Donnell, who was the highest civilian official of the Federal government locally and whose office was responsible for the registration, announced that "...the JACL is providing interpreters for Japanese-alien registration and in other ways aiding in the registration."

On February 16, 1942, the *Issei* living in and around Piedras Blancas north of San Simeon were relocated. On February 18, the *T-T* reported that 20 "aliens"—Japanese—had been rounded up by the San Luis Obispo Sheriff in the Oso Flaco area of the south county. These *Issei* were taken to a relocation station in Santa Barbara. The article quoted Sheriff Murray C. Hathaway as saying that "...little or no contraband had been uncovered in (the morning raid in) San Luis Obispo County."

Despite these "raids" portending eventual relocation of all Japanese, citizen and non-citizen alike, the JACL continued its policy of cooperation with law enforcement and Federal agencies. On February 20, 1942, the *T-T* reported that James Nakamura, secretary of the local JACL, had offered to conduct a survey of *Nisei* visits to Japan and to give this information to Federal officials. Some later observers felt that the JACL had gone too far in its efforts to prove the patriotism of Japanese-Americans.

In October of 1944, an official of the War Relocation Authority, in a report on the San Luis Obispo area, asserted: "The JACL came into some ill repute when it advised farmers just outside the prohibited zone to keep on with their farming (in this case, early spring plantings), only to have the evacuation axe fall."

The War Relocation Authority official went on to report: "Some executive officers of the JACL were also looked upon with suspicion as the ones who were responsible for the detention of prominent *Isseis*." The latter accusation may be untrue, but certainly many Japanese farmers did, indeed, go ahead with their planting.

Spring plantings were to be ill fated, not only for the Japanese-Americans who owned their own land, but most especially for those who held leased land. On February 21, 1942, the *T-T* observed that "most of the land under cultivation by Japanese in this county is on a lease or share arrangement." The journal said that "already the Japanese of the county are endeavoring to sell their homes and properties with as little loss as possible. Leases on vegetable lands are being terminated and plans for leaving the area are under way."

As it happened, the majority of the Japanese residents who held leased—rather than personally owned—land would never return to the county. And by 1945, when some Japanese came back, the total number of *Issei* and *Nisei* in San Luis Obispo County was reduced by at least 85 percent.

But in 1942, there were concerns that transcended economics: Young *Nisei* were worried about their *Issei* parents.

The Los Osos family of Masaji Eto was a case in point. Masaji was a *Nisei*, but his father had been arrested on December 7, 1941, under F.B.I. orders, despite the senior Eto being cited as a prominent resident of the county in the most recent historical account of the county written by State Senator Chris Jespersen in 1939. Now, Masaji, being the only son in the family, was placed in a position of total responsibility for his family's well being. With the alien evacuation order, his mother, Take Eto, had to be separated from the family to a point east of State Highway 1. Masaji found housing off Grand Avenue in San Luis Obispo for his mother. This was only the beginning of a rapid sequence of moves for the Eto family.

Shortly after moving his mother into San Luis Obispo, and hence east of Highway 1, Masaji was confronted with Executive Order 9066. Initially this order was interpreted by many *Nisei* as meaning removal from the coastal areas of California. Masaji Eto leased his family's Los Osos Valley farm to a neighbor, Joe Turri, with whom the family had worked closely over the years. There wasn't much time to prepare for the move, so the Etos could only ask a nominal rent. But in this regard, they were far more fortunate than Japanese who did not own their own farms, for these leaseholders had to give up everything, unless they held a very long-term lease on highly favorable terms.

Masaji Eto moved his family to a small farm just west of U.S. Highway 99 near the town of Tulare. The family had barely settled in when they were told by government officials that anything west of Highway 99 was considered as being within the prohibited zone under the interpretation of Executive Order 9066. Once again the Eto family had to relocate, this time to Porterville near the Sierra foothills in Tulare County. By May or June of 1942, Masaji recalls, his family was told that another move was in order—this time to one of the ten "camps" that had been set up by the War Relocation Authority in Arizona, Colorado, Idaho, Utah, Wyoming and Arkansas and in two of the most desolate areas of California: Tule Lake in Modoc County and Manzanar in the volcanic-ash-swept high plains of Inyo County.

The Eto family had begun planting spring crops in Los Osos when they were compelled to "relocate." In Porterville, they had set in a summer crop of tomatoes that they had to leave behind. Now they were told that they would be taken to a spot they had never heard of: Poston, Arizona.

Masaji Eto's sister, Toshiko, was an honors graduate of Mills College in Oakland and of the Stanford University School of Nursing in San Francisco. By early March of 1942, Toshiko had accepted a position as camp nurse at Manzanar. Rather than have his family split up, Masaji requested and received permission from the War Relocation Authority to move with his recent bride, Margaret, three of his sisters and his mother, Take, to that camp on the eastern side of the Sierra Nevada.

In a 1980 interview in the *T-T*, Masaji Eto told staff writer Ann Fairbanks, "I didn't want to go very far away from home...I always had the feeling I would be able to come back, because the American people are very fair."

Even before Executive Order 9066 went into effect, many county residents were aware of its consequences for holders of leased land. On February 21, 1942, the *T-T* observed that "most of the land under cultivation by Japanese in the county is on lease or share agreement" and that "leases on vegetable lands are being terminated and plans for leaving the area are under way."

On February 25, 1942, Parker Talbot, County Farm Adviser, said that "land use surveys conducted here have shown that most county farms are too small for adequate farm income," and he pointed out that "removal of the Japanese will return lands to the original farm units." Informed mem-

ETO FAMILY ALBUM

Tameji Eto, left, with his wife, Take, and her sister and brother-in-law, Mr. and Mrs. Mizusaki. Taken on Easter day, 1941, at the Eto home in Los Osos.

The Eto family, back row, from left: Mary, Masaji, Tameji, Susie. Front row; Nancy, Grace and Alice.

Nancy and Grace at their Los Osos home. Nancy's husband served in the U.S. Military Intelligence Service during World War II and the Korean Conflict. Grace's husband, Yoshimi Shibata, served in the U.S. Army during World War II.

Mary, left, at age 16 with Susie, age 14.

Toshiko Eto attended Stanford Nursing School. During the re-location years, she practiced her skills at Manzanar.

Leo Kikuchi, Susie Eto's husband, and their son, Ronald. Leo gave his life for the United States on an Italian battlefield as a soldier in the U.S. Army 442nd, the most decorated unit in the war. Ronald served his country in France.

A gathering at the Eto home. From left: Susie, holding her son, Ronald; Mary; Take (the girls' mother); and Margaret, Masaji's wife. Masaji and Margaret's son, Alan, served a tour of duty with the U.S. Army in Vietnam. Of that experience he says, "It was a scary time, but I wanted to do my part...even though, as the sole surviving son of a farm family, I couldn't be compelled to go."

Photos courtesy of Susie Eto Kikuchi Bauman and Grace Eto Shibata.

Harry Nuss, manager of the Bank of Italy/Bank of America, was a good friend to the Japanese community. *Photo courtesy of Dorian Willett.*

bers of the county were clearly aware of the long-term effects of the evacuation order: A major demographic reshuffling was going to be an inevitable consequence.

The Japanese-American Citizens League also apparently acknowledged the inevitability of this population shift. On March 16, 1942, the *T-T* reported that 75 members of the JACL had met at the Buddhist Temple and had reacted favorably to a proposal "that the San Luis Obispo area Japanese colony move en masse to form a new colony inland."

The JACL was capitulating to the mood of the time which was reflected in the *T-T* editorial of February 20, 1942: "Arrest of enemy aliens in San Luis Obispo (County) this week is heartening news to Americans of this area who foresee a long, hard war and possible Jap raids on the West Coast." The Japanese-American community in San Luis Obispo County had given up any possibility of staying; survival as a community was obviously the new game plan. Much of the oral testimony collected both in this county and in other areas of the Pacific Coast reveals a common pattern. Initially, most of the *Issei* accepted rumors that only non-citizens would be evacuated.

Then came the big shock, as newspapers announced that all persons of Japanese descent were to be evacuated. There was an air of disbelief, especially with the short notice. But disbelief quickly turned into resignation and acceptance.

This sequence of reactions to the wartime crisis does much to explain the somewhat controversial role of the JACL in cooperating with authorities in rounding up radios and registering *Issei*. Many third and fourth generation Japanese-Americans have criticized their *Issei* parents and grandparents for being too passive.

But that hindsight view ignores the historical milieu of 1941.

Take the case of Los Angeles businessman George Aratani. The Aratanis operated a wholesale produce business in Santa Maria. The family had financed the Santa Maria High School's basketball team's trip to Japan just prior to the war. George Aratani went through the evacuation experience. In 1981 he described what he felt in February of 1942: "We couldn't believe it at first...It's strange, but when there's a war on and all your Caucasian buddies are being drafted, you're sort of resigned to the fact that it's because of the war. You just accept it because a law is a law and you've got to obey."

The Japanese had an almost unblemished record with law enforcement agencies throughout the United States. The community leaders were not about to permit that tradition to be broken in reaction to the paranoia of their neighbors or the evacuation order.

Gordon Bennett recalls the evacuation of Japanese families from the Arroyo Grande Valley: "After the first part of 1942, the Japanese were sent to internment camps in the San Joaquin Valley. Many of the Japanese in the

San Luis Obispo Japanese baseball team. Front row, from left: Pat Nagano, unidentified player, "Lefty" Nishijima and Imao Hori. Second row, Ben Tsutsumi and William Nagano (in suit). *Photo courtesy of Lillian Nishijima Sakurai.*

Arroyo Grande area reported to the Arroyo Grande High School, where they were loaded on several buses and were taken to an internment camp near Tulare. I can still vividly remember the local Japanese people boarding the buses in front of our home on Crown Hill. The Army had soldiers there armed with shotguns, a very grim sight to see your friends go through."

Compliance with the law often meant more than economic hardship. While the War Relocation Authority tried to avoid splitting up families, special circumstances often made this necessary.

The family of Kazuo Ikeda of Arroyo Grande faced a unique situation. Shortly after Pearl Harbor, Kazuo's father was in a farming accident and was paralyzed. Since the family farm was on the Oceano side of Highway 1, the Ikeda family had to pack and move to the Japanese school grounds which contained several homes. Two or three other families moved with the Ikedas into this compound. Later, when the order to move east of Highway 99 came, the other families departed, but Kazuo was unable to move his father. Kazuo's family eventually was sent to the Tulare assembly center, but he remained in Arroyo Grande to care for his ailing parent.

The authorities knew the elder Ikeda could not be moved, and there was no hospital at the assembly center. Kazuo was given a special permit to stay and take care of his father. So, for the next two and one-half months, Kazuo and his father lived in the home of Mr. and Mrs. Vard Loomis. The Ikedas were permitted a three-mile radius in which they could move, enabling them to travel from the Loomis home to the hospital where Kazuo's father received treatments to their farm in the lower Arroyo Grande.

After that period, the relocation authorities sent Kazuo a letter indicating that facilities were now available for his father at the assembly center in Tulare. Arrangements were being made for an ambulance to transport the father and son from Arroyo Grande to Tulare. Kazuo was instructed to go to San Luis Obispo to pick up the necessary papers. As Kazuo drove from the Loomis home, the military police followed him and reported an Oriental driving a car into San Luis Obispo. An arrest order was sent to the sheriff's department, and Kazuo was taken to county jail. Despite the fact that he held the appropriate permits for travel and was known by the arresting officers, Kazuo was not released until the military authorities from Camp San Luis Obispo investigated the matter.

At Tulare, Kazuo was told that he and his brothers were to be sent to the relocation center at Gila, Arizona. Because the camp lacked a hospital, his father and mother were to be sent to the Fresno assembly center until adequate preparations for hospital care for the father could be made at the Gila camp. So, once again, the family was separated. The senior Ikeda passed away the summer after he was transferred to Gila.

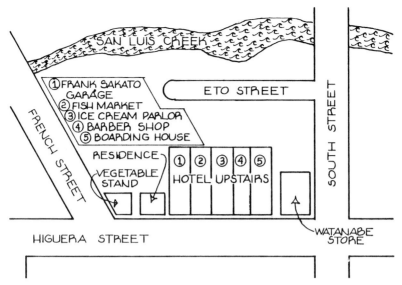

Map of Japanese commercial center in San Luis Obispo. Eto Street received its name, after prominent citizen Tameji Eto, in 1931. The street was renamed Brook Street in March, 1942, by the San Luis Obispo City Council. *Map drawn by Alison Bryan.*

The Sakamoto family was interned for awhile at Delano, then the family was sent to Poston, Arizona. Frank Sakamoto was forced to interrupt his freshman year at Cal Poly.

Walter Tanaka, brother of Helen Foree Keller's student Lucy Tanaka, now lives in San Jose, California. (His recollections of training at Camp Roberts appear elsewhere in this volume.) The depression of the 1930s had badly hurt his family's income from leased land just south of San Luis Obispo. He had to drop out of school for four years. Then, after an illness, he returned to San Luis Obispo High School to graduate in the class of 1940. He was drafted into the Army in 1941.

Tanaka's father had once served as president of the Japanese Association and was arrested early in 1942 by Federal authorities as a "prominent *Issei* leader." Later, while Walter was serving in the Army at Camp Savage, Minnesota, his family was sent to the internment camp at Poston, Arizona.

William Nagano, the eldest son in a Morro Bay farm family, was drafted in February of 1941. He served in the United States Army in the general services branch throughout the war. Both Patrick and George Nagano later enlisted in the Army.

Among the *Nisei* from San Luis Obispo County who served during the war were Haruyuki Kuranaga, Toshio Nakamura, Munetoshi G. Horiuchi, Takashi Yukitake, Tosh Sadahiro, Saburo Ikeda, Walter Tanaka, Hilo Fuchiwaki, Tadashi Otani and Fujio Kobara, according to a list supplied to us by Masaji Eto. Walter Tanaka remembers that Bill Kuroda and Fukuo Maruyama, both of Pismo Beach, and Akira Tsutsumi also served in the U.S.

military during the war. Most of these soldiers did not return to San Luis Obispo County to live.

But more on their wartime exploits and the sagas of their families in volume two of *War Comes to the Middle Kingdom*.

Meanwhile, a sad denouement to the Japanese Odyssey in San Luis Obispo took place on February 24, 1942. The San Luis Obispo City Council drafted Ordinance number 236 (New Series) for the purpose of "CHANGING THE OFFICIAL NAME OF ETO STREET."

In a pique of wartime hysteria, the council moved that:

"The name of that certain street now known as and officially named Eto Street, in the Nippon Tracts according to the official map of said tract on file in the office of the County Recorder of the County of San Luis Obispo, which street extends for approximately one block Southerly from South Street, is hereby changed, and said street shall hereafter be known, named and designated as Brook Street."

The motion passed unanimously.

It was as though the city council and many of the citizens wished to erase the lives and contributions of the Japanese in San Luis Obispo.

Dan and Liz Krieger

BASEBALL AND THE GOOD NEIGHBOR POLICY

"**C**ome on over. I'm just listening to the baseball game on the radio!" exclaimed Gladys Loomis.

Baseball and Gladys go way back.

Eighty-one year old Gladys Loomis has always been a live wire. She is interested in everything. "Every time I saw a need, I jumped in: Boy Scouts, Camp Fire, helping found Cuesta College and now lots of work towards the goal of a South County Performing Arts Center."

During the depths of the Depression, Gladys tackled Russian and Greek at the University of California, Berkeley. For a while, she tried to please her father by studying law.

There she was, one of five women and 85 men in a criminal law class at Cal's Boalt Hall. The professor called upon her to begin the recitation dealing with a rape case. Gladys recalls her feelings: "I had never heard the word 'rape' in public and wasn't sure what it meant. I guess that I had been over protected."

Gladys convinced her parents and the Dean of the Graduate Division at Cal to permit her to transfer out of the Law School and into a regular graduate program. That change led to her becoming a teacher. In 1932, she arrived at the 150 pupil Arroyo Grande High School as a teacher of drama, speech, English and physical education.

She met her future husband, Vard Loomis, at a card party. Whist was the preferred game in Arroyo Grande in 1932. But a powerful team was formed at those whist parties. Vard had just graduated from Stanford, where he'd been president of the class of 1931. A series of deaths in the Loomis family had left Vard as the one most responsible for running the family business.

E.C. Loomis and Company had a wide and varied clientele. The Loomises especially valued their Japanese-American customers. The farm supply company invited Japanese farmers from throughout the Central Coast, the Bay Area and the Los Angeles Basin to picnics in Lopez Canyon— now covered by Lopez Lake.

Gladys appreciatively recalls how the Japanese taught them to make salad in washtubs for the big barbecues. It was made with cabbage, green pepper, celery and shrimp or crab. And it was delicious.

The Arroyo Grande baseball team in 1936. The team was coached by Vard Loomis, a special friend to the Japanese community. On the left is Kazuo's father, Juzo Ikeda. *Photo courtesy of Kazuo Ikeda.*

The Loomis family developed many close personal ties to the Japanese farmers in the Pismo Beach-Arroyo Grande region. In the years just before the war, Gladys' husband, Vard Loomis, was asked to coach the all-Japanese baseball team. Vard had been a star pitcher on Stanford's "nine" during the late 1920s.

The team played "away" games against other all-Japanese teams in Santa Maria, Santa Barbara, Bakersfield, Fresno and San Jose. Vard would drive and Gladys would travel along. She remembers how the team always liked to eat at Chinese restaurants.

The Japanese Fishing Club invited Vard to go with them. He became their "designated driver," allowing the club members to enjoy their sake.

On New Year's Day, the entire Loomis family would gather at the Hayashi Farm in Arroyo Grande's Cienega District. The Loomises would join the Hayashis in making traditional Japanese rice cakes.

Haru "Harry" Hayashi was best man for John Loomis and Gordon Bennett. Many years after the war, Pat Kawaguchi was best man at the wedding of Vard and Gladys' son, Terry.

Gladys taught many Japanese students. Among them was Karl Taku, who later headed the Japanese-American Citizens League.

When the Japanese were evacuated, Ivan, Buster and Vard Loomis leased and farmed the Fukahara farm in order to preserve it for their friends. The Fukaharas had just built a beautiful five-bedroom home on their farm. This was probably the nicest farmhouse on any of the Japanese ranches.

Vard and Gladys were special friends to the Ikeda family. When war broke out, the elder Ikeda was incapacitated by a broken back, requiring private nursing around the clock. Since he was too ill to be relocated in March, 1942, Kazuo, his eldest son stayed with him. Later, he was transferred to the small, old Arroyo Grande Hospital near Traffic Way. The War

Relocation Authorities permitted Kazuo to live with Vard and Gladys, so that he could be nearby his ailing father. Kazuo would babysit Vard and Gladys' eighteen-month old daughter, Sandy.

Gladys remembers the Sheriff searching the Loomis home for short-wave radios because of Kazuo's presence. Kazuo was once stopped by the police for driving with a young white woman in the car. Gladys had asked Kazuo to drive the girl home.

Gladys also recalls with distaste how a longtime customer stormed into the E.C. Loomis store one day. Buster, Vard's older brother, was watching the store from a cot. He was critically ill from the effects of rheumatic fever. The man went up to Buster's bed and shouted, "You Jap lovers...if you don't quit, I am going to burn your store down!"

Gladys is proud to proclaim the truth of the matter confirmed by F.B.I. reports: "Never once was any disloyalty found in our county. Nearly all of the young men who played on Vard's *Nisei* baseball team who were of draft age volunteered immediately. Not one was drafted. Almost all of them worked in military intelligence because they were bilingual. Some served in the 442 Infantry Combat Unit, the most decorated American unit of the war."

Gladys also recalls the sad story of the Kawaoka family. The elder Kawaoka was, according to Gladys, "probably the most important Japanese resident of the South county." He was a resident of Hawaii in 1898. He automatically was granted American citizenship when Hawaii became an American territory.

Rather than accept the humiliation of relocation, Mr. Kawaoka decided to accept the option of being sent to Japan along with the Japanese citizens who were scheduled for repatriation.

Meanwhile, Yosh Kawaoka, his son, served in the United States Army Intelligence under General MacArthur. After the war, he moved to Japan to be near his family. Today Yosh heads his own steel company.

In 1980 the *California Nisei Baseball Association* played their series in Arroyo Grande. They dedicated their program to Vard Loomis.

Shortly thereafter, the Ikeda family placed a housing subdivision on their land. They named one of the two streets, "Vard Loomis Way."

Vard died in 1979, but Gladys still plugs away at their "Good Neighbor Policy" in her friendly, unpretentious way.

This story first appeared in the Telegram-Tribune *on September 28, 1991.*

REFERENCES FOR ODYSSEY

Aratani, George. Former resident of Santa Maria quoted in Stacey Peck, "Home question & answer: Sakaye & George Aratani," *Home* magazine supplement, *Los Angeles Times*, November 1, 1981, p.25.

Avila, Josephine Garcia and Frank Avila, October 4, 1981, interview with Liz and Dan Krieger.

Bauman, Susie Eto Kikuchi. September 30, 1991, interview with Liz Krieger.

Bosworth, Allan R. *America's Concentration Camps*. New York: Norton, 1967.

Brown, Robert R.. September 30, 1981 interview with Liz and Dan Krieger.

Chuman, Frank F. *The Bamboo People*. Del Mar, California: Publisher's, Inc., 1976.

DeWitt, John L. "Final Report: Japanese Evacuation from the West Coast." Washington: U.S. Government Printing Office, 1943.

Eto, Masaji and Margaret. May 11, 1981, and October 10, 1991, interviews with Liz and Dan Krieger.

Fairbanks, Ann. "Osos farmer reflects on war hysteria." *Telegram-Tribune*, October 9, 1980, p. A-8. An interview with Masaji Eto.

Fisher, L.H. "History of Contract Labor in California Agriculture," in *The Harvest Labor Market in California*. Cambridge, Mass.: Harvard University Press, 1953.

Fukunaga, Kofuji Eto daughter of Tamejii Eto. Transcription of tape made by Kofuji Fukunaga April 17, 1964. San Luis Obispo County Historical Society Tape Collection, San Luis Obispo County Museum.

Grodzins, Morton. *Americans Betrayed: Politics and the Japanese Evacuation*. Chicago: University of Chicago Press, 1949.

Ito, K. *Issei: A History of Japanese Immigrants in North America*. Seattle: Japanese Community Service, 1973.

Jesperson, Chris N. *History of San Luis Obispo County*. San Luis Obispo, Ca.: Harold McLean Meier, 1939. pp.222-224. Jesperson says: "The distinction of being the first Japanese citizen to establish residence belongs to Tamezi [sic] Eto, prominent horticulturist, who, by his science and enterprise, has done much to extend the fame of San Luis Obispo County throughout all parts of the state."

Keller, Helen Foree. September 16, 1981, interview with Liz and Dan Krieger.

Kitano, H.H.L. *Japanese Americans: The Evolution of a Subculture*. Englewood Cliffs, N.J.: Prentice-Hall, 1976.

Kurokawa, Paul and Betty. October 14, 1981; February 11, 1982; January 17, 1984; March 11, 1986 interviews with Liz and Dan Krieger.

Loomis, Gladys. September 22, 1991 interview with Liz and Dan Krieger.

Matsuura, Shinobu. *Higan: Compassionate Vow: Selected Writings of Shinobu Matsuura*. English edition translated by the Matsuura Family from the original Higan, edited by Souke Nishimoto (Kyoto, Japan: Dobosha, 1972). Matsuura was the founder of the Children's Home and Japanese School in Guadalupe, California.

Myer, Dillon S. *Uprooted Americans*. Tucson: University of Arizona Press, 1971. Myer succeeded Milton Eisenhower as Director of the War Relocation Authority in June of 1942.

Nagano, Patrick. September 16, 1981 interview with Liz and Dan Krieger. .

Parrish, Frieda Boysen. October 1, 1981, interview with Liz and Dan Krieger.

Sakamoto, Mitsu and Yotsu. August 11, 1991, interview with Liz Krieger.

Sakurai, Kiyoshi and Lillian, January 1991 interviews with Liz and Dan Krieger.

San Luis Obispo County Telegram-Tribune, 1939-1945.

Shibata, Grace Eto. "Okaasan (Mother)," in *Japanese American Women, Three Generations, 1890-1900*. Nakano, Mei T., Ming Press, 1990.

Tachibana, Yoshiko, et al., "Oral Histories of Japanese Americans in San Luis Obispo County," Library, California Polytechnic State University, San Luis Obispo, Senior Project in Liberal Studies/Education, 1981: (1) Interview with Stone Saruwatari, March 2, 1980, by Ashley Green; (2) Interview with Shigechika Kobara, January 5, 1980, by Ricardo Medina; (3) Interview with Isoko Fuchiwaki by Yoshiko Tachibana. These oral interviews were conducted under the direction of Art Hansen, visiting professor of history at Cal Poly from Cal State Fullerton.

Taku, Karl. February 11, 1988, interview with Dan Krieger.

Tanaka, Walter. October 12, 1981; September 9, 1982; July 4, 1985 interviews with Liz and Dan Krieger.

Thomsen, Eric H. "War Relocation Authority, Santa Barbara District: Final Report." Santa Barbara: United States Department of the Interior, War Relocation Authority, January 30, 1946.

Tudor, E.O. "Swede". August 19, 1981 interview with Liz and Dan Krieger. Mr. Tudor was an employee of Union Oil Company in San Luis Obispo in 1941-45. He expressed his personal concern at the time for the plight of the Japanese farmers who were long-time residents.

United States Department of the Interior, War Relocation Authority, Community Analysis Section, October, 1942: Locality Study No. 5: San Luis Obispo County and Environs-Highlights of Evacuation.

GLOSSARY

Anschluss—A German word for "union," referring to the incorporation of Austria into Hitler's German Empire on March 13, 1938. The Nazis forced the resignation of Austrian Chancellor Kurt Schusnigg and replaced him with the pro-Nazi Seyss-Inquart who, by a prearranged agreement, invited Germany to occupy Austria.

Battle of the Bulge—German counteroffensive into the Ardennes Forest in Belgium, December 16-30, 1944. As the center of the Anglo-American Allies' line fell back, a "bulge" was created. Thus Nazi Germany's last significant thrust to the west was named "the Battle of the Bulge."

Buchenwald—One of the most notorious of the German death camps employed in Hitler's "Final Solution." The camps were originally used for political and "racial" enemies of the Third Reich. The Nazis employed slave labor and performed sadistic medical experiments here.

Fascism—A set of nationalist, authoritarian, anticommunist, antiliberal political beliefs typified by the Fascist Party founded by Benito Mussolini in Italy in 1919. Both the political party and the ideology derive their name from the Latin word *fasces*—the bundle of birch rods wrapped around a headman's axe which was the ancient Roman symbol of state authority.

Mussolini came to power on an anti-*Bolshevick* (Leninist-Stalinist) platform. he claimed to be neither capitalist nor socialist. Instead he said that a fascist state incorporated the well being of all citizens. Hence the term "Corporate State" is usually applied to Fascist states. In fact the overwhelming characteristic was the adulation of Mussolini, who took the title *Il Duce* (the leader) and was greeted by his followers with the slogan "Mussolini is Always Right."

Initially, Adolf Hitler mimicked many of Mussolini's ideas. So too did the *Falange* party of Francisco Franco in Spain after 1936.

Fifth Column—Secret enemy sympathizers who might rise from within a country or a region to assist the attackers. The term was first coined by the *Falangist* General Mola during the Spanish Civil War (1936-39). He was showing the world's press a map of his four military columns advancing on Madrid. He claimed to have a "Fifth Column" within the city itself which would insure victory.

The term acquired wide usage, 1939-41, first as Hitler's armies poured into Poland, Norway, Belgium, France and Russia, and then apropros of the Japanese attack on Pearl Harbor.

Gestapo—German acronym for *Geheime Staatspolizei*—the Secret State Police established in the German state of Prussia by Hermann Goering on April 26, 1933. It replaced the Prussian political police. It became an instrument of terror against opponents of the Nazi regime. In April, 1934, the *Gestapo* was rapidly expanded throughout the Third Reich by Heinrich Himmler. It eventually became an arm of the *SS* or *Schutzstaffen* (guards detachment).

Issei—Japanese immigrants to the United States or its territories who were denied citizenship until 1952.

Kristallnacht—"The Night of Broken Glass:" Nazi inspired anti-Jewish pogrom which destroyed Jewish shops, homes and synagogues in German cities and towns, November 9-10, 1938. The streets were littered with broken glass or *kristal*. A massive amount of damage was done. Many thousands of Jews were imprisoned by the *Gestapo*. Hundreds of others were brutally attacked in the streets. Hitler added insult to injury by fining German Jews for the damage to "German property."

Maginot Line—Elaborate French fortications including tunnels, rail lines, elevators and ventilation systems, stretching from Luxembourg to Belgium along France's eastern frontier, intended to prevent a German invasion. The overconfident French thought it was impregnable, but in May-June 1940, the German blitzkrieg (lightning war) by-passed it by crossing through neutral Belgium.

Mischling—A person of "mixed blood" or "partly Jewish ancestry" under Germany's notorious Nuremburg Laws of 1935. These racial laws codified Nazi theories of race, denied Jews German citizenship and forbade them to marry Aryans. It was a prelude to the systematic murder of nearly six million Jews in the concentration camps.

Nazi—Generic term for a member of Adolf Hitler's *Nationalsozialitische Deutsche Arbeiter Partei* (German National Socialist Workers Party) which governed Germany from January 30, 1933, until the surrender of Germany in 1945.

Hitler's Nazi Party doctrines and practices were extreme variants of Benito Mussolini's Fascist Party. It was tainted by the anti-Semitic, racialist doctrines of Aryan superiority.

Nisei—First generation of Japanese-Americans born in the United States. By virtue of their birth, they were United States citizens.

Swastika—an ancient religious symbol in the shape of a hooked or "broken" cross. It is linked with the revival of interest in Germanic legends at the end of the 19th century. The word *swastika* is derived from the ancient Sanskrit word for well-being or luck. Adolf Hitler adopted it as the emblem of National Socialism (Nazism) in the 1920s. In September, 1935, the *swastika* became Germany's national emblem.

Vichy France—The southeastern half of France which was not occupied by the Nazis after the French surrender in June, 1940. It gets its name from the provincial French spa town where Marshal Phillip Pétain established the interim capital in July, 1940. The Vichy regime was dictatorial and followed the Nazi policy of anti-Semitism. Vichy actively collaborated with the Nazis after November, 1942.

INDEX

To be continued...

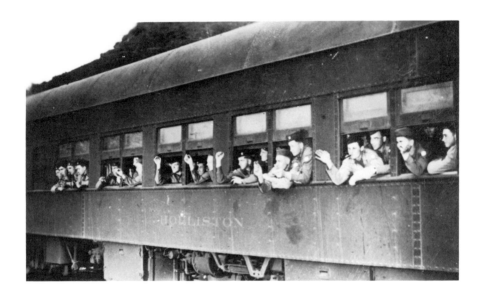

Stand by for Volume II of

WAR
COMES TO THE MIDDLE KINGDOM
1942-1945

scheduled for release during late 1992.